DISAVOWED

C. G. COOPER

"DISAVOWED"

Book 8 of the Corps Justice Series
Copyright © 2014, 2018 C. G. Cooper Entertainment. All Rights Reserved
Author: C. G. Cooper
(http://www.cg-cooper.com)

GET A FREE COPY OF THE CORPS JUSTICE PREQUEL SHORT STORY, *GOD-SPEED*, JUST FOR SUBSCRIBING AT CG-COOPER.COM

Warning: This story is intended for mature audiences and contains profanity and violence.

Dedications

To my loyal group of *Novels Live* warriors, thanks for your help in crafting this novel.
To our amazing troops serving all over the world, thank you for your bravery and service.
Semper Fidelis

CORPS JUSTICE OATH BY COL. CALVIN STOKES, SR. (USMC, RET.)

1. We will protect and defend the Constitution of the United States.
2. We will protect the weak and punish the wicked.
3. When the laws of this nation hinder the completion of these duties, our moral compass will guide us to see the mission through.

* * *

Si Vis Pacem, Para Iustitiam: In order to have peace, you must first have justice.

HELMAND PROVINCE, AFGHANISTAN

9:12AM, AUGUST 23RD

It was a game. At regular intervals throughout the day an old Afghan would unchain the rickety wood slat door. He would peer in with one rheumy eye through a hole in the door, then open it. Always careful. His gnarled and heavily tanned arm reaching in to place a dented aluminum tray on the concrete floor. It held a plate covered with a dented metal dome.

Sometimes the covered plate contained a bottle of water, a piece of bread and a scrap of stringy meat. Goat meat. It was the other times that his captors had their fun.

The second time he'd reached for the tray, relishing the thought of a sip of water, he'd almost dropped the metal top in surprise. Lying on the cracked earthen plate was a severed hand, fresh blood pooled like a bed of soup.

The time after that they'd given him an ear. Then, earlier that morning, he'd found out where the parts were coming from. When he'd uncovered the plate he found the head of a man he knew, his eyes bulging from his final death throes. Not a man. Almost a boy.

Ikram was a nineteen year old Afghan he'd recruited weeks before. The boy had a knack for languages and had helped his employer master the local Pashtun dialect. They'd often stayed up well into the night, Ikram pronouncing words for his friend, always patient.

He'd learned that Ikram was a tenth son, the youngest. While his brothers and sisters chose to stay close to their ancestral home, Ikram left for a shot at seeing the world. They'd met by chance in a small cafe where Ikram was waiting tables. He'd surprised the foreigner with his mastery of English and the two had struck up a conversation until the cafe owner yelled for the boy to get back to work.

The memories of their time together played over in his mind as he'd looked down at the young man's contorted face. By the jagged and ripped look of the neck wound they'd butchered him alive. Ikram had felt every cut. He said a silent prayer for the boy.

Major Bartholomew Andrews, USMC, Andy to his friends, sat in the corner of the ramshackle room picking at a scab on the back of his hand. He'd been captured days before. Time ground by as if accompanied by a maddening dirge. Memories spun. The rest of his team slaughtered in a dank alley. At the time, Ikram and Maj. Andrews were the only ones left standing. There'd been time for one last phone call, to the only person Andy knew he could trust.

After the satellite phone had been knocked from his hand, he'd taken down six until someone threw a concussion grenade and knocked him unconscious. It was the last time he'd seen Ikram until uncovering the gruesome platter.

The game aside, no one had touched him. He'd awakened to find himself in the room he now occupied, shackled to the stone wall by ancient iron manacles strapped to his wrists and ankles. They clanked together as he tried to shift into a more comfortable position. Impossible. Sleep came in waves.

Although his body ached and his throat screamed from thirst, Andy's mind analyzed the situation, searching, calculating. Something wasn't right. If he was the target of a kidnapping, why the games? Why didn't they torture him, try to get information out of him?

The lack of physical abuse worried him more than if he'd been strapped to a wooden beam and beaten until he broke.

Andy held no illusions about his ability to outlast interrogation. He was a Marine infantry officer. He was a Navy Cross winner. He knew the horrors of war and the price paid for victory.

But he also knew that eventually everyone cracked. The trick was to hang on as long as you could and hope that you'd either escape or get rescued. Death was the only other obvious alternative. The problem for Andy was two-fold. First, he was in possession of troves of classified information. His time in Afghanistan had been well spent. Second, no one knew where he was. This was his mission, the first he'd been allowed to plan and execute while on loan to the CIA. There was no oversight. He was on his own.

He'd handpicked his team. Three former American special forces soldiers plus him and Ikram. Small. Mobile. Undetectable.

It was as if he'd given the attackers a detailed description of the operation, from timelines to check points. He remembered the hairs on the back of his neck standing at attention as soon as they'd landed. He should have listened to the warning and aborted the mission. It was pride that pushed him forward, ignoring the alarm bells in his head.

But how had they known? No one knew the details of the

op except for Andy and he'd burned the notes before leaving Camp Leatherneck. How had they found him? And, more importantly, why were they keeping him alive?

His thoughts rattled as the chains on the door creaked open, another tray set on the cracked concrete floor.

UNIVERSITY OF VIRGINIA

Kyle Hazlitt was a third year student at the University of Virginia. A red-shirt walk-on for UVa's football team, Hazlitt felt the constant need to keep himself conditioned. If he wanted to keep his hard fought position as #2 wide receiver, he'd have to work for it. Even though there'd already been morning practice, he was back to lifting at Memorial Gym.

Just having drained the last of his gallon jug of water, the college wide-out walked to the water fountain to get a refill. He passed one of the private rooms where he occasionally stretched on the wrestling mats. A large figure flew past the window. *What the...?*

Hazlitt moved to the door and watched as two men charged at each other. It looked like an unfair fight. The one he'd seen run by the window was a huge black guy. He figured the man had to be close to seven feet tall and was built like an NFL lineman.

The other guy was white and more than a foot shorter

than his partner. He was trim where the other guy was muscle bound and hulking. Despite the size difference, the smaller guy didn't seem to care. He bulled in, diving and rolling at the last possible moment, narrowly missing the hands of the giant with the flat top.

He watched as they circled each other, both men smiling, soaked in sweat. Like two combatants in a mixed martial arts ring, they maneuvered around each other, sometimes grasping a leg or arm of their opponent, but each always twisting away. To Hazlitt's surprise the smaller guy was holding his own. He couldn't tell how, but it looked to be a subtle shift here or a quick slip there.

The big guy finally got the brown-haired guy on the ground and flipped him around, getting him to tap-out with an arm-bar. Hazlitt shook his head and continued on. He wouldn't want to take on either of those guys.

* * *

MASTER SERGEANT WILLY TRENT, USMC (RETIRED), helped his boss up. Cal Stokes grinned up at his friend.

"I thought I had you, Top."

Trent shook his head and laughed, the sound deep and rumbling. "How many times do I have to tell you, Cal? I cannot be beaten!" He stood with his hands on his hips like a kid wearing a red cape pretending he was Superman.

Cal chuckled. "You know, you do have me by like a hundred pounds."

Trent shrugged. "Tell that to Royce Gracie. Dude took out guys bigger than me in UFC One."

Cal shook his head. "Fine. You win."

"Now, was that so hard?"

Cal gave Trent the middle finger, but smiled as he grabbed a towel off his gym bag. He didn't like to lose, ever. But he guessed that if he had to, he might as well lose to one of his best friends who was possibly the strongest man he'd ever met. Even during his time in the Marine Corps, Cal had never met anyone who could manhandle the formidable MSgt Trent.

TEN MINUTES LATER, THEY WALKED INTO THE RENOVATED home that housed their budding corporate headquarters. Situated on the corner of Rugby Road and Preston Avenue, The Jefferson Group owned properties on two corners of the intersection. The second property was still under construction, so they were walking in to the recently finished 'pentagon' property, named for the shape of the lot.

On paper, The Jefferson Group was a small consultancy that sourced its highly qualified principals to private corporations and the federal government. They even gave the occasional guest lecture at the University.

While Cal Stokes was the de facto leader of the small company, billionaire Jonas Layton was its face. Layton had made his billions in the tech industry. By using his genius level brain to build software widely adopted by multi-national corporations, and his uncanny ability to predict future events, Layton was increasingly being called "The Fortuneteller" by industry insiders. His prognosticative powers were becoming legendary.

Layton dealt with the day-to-day minutia of running a business. Although Cal was still majority owner of Stokes Security International (SSI), a private security company founded by his father, Marine Col. Calvin Stokes, Sr., he now handled The Jefferson Group's burgeoning covert division.

Months before, he'd left SSI and been tasked by his good friend, U.S. President Brandon Zimmer, to form a new entity. This secret endeavor would have a public face but a very private mission. The Navy Cross winner was given the opportunity to be the president's secret weapon. He'd done it for years with SSI, but now he had a better cover. So while local police and government agencies battled bureaucracy and fickle lawmakers, Cal and his team of operators at The Jefferson Group were free to battle the hidden forces that were attacking America.

Just days before, the team had returned from overseas where Cal had directed the complete destruction of the budding terror organization called ISIS. Through careful coordination with American and coalition military assets, the president's men conducted a shock and awe campaign that was now pursuing global terrorists back to their homes. The gloves were off. America was playing for keeps, and Cal and his team were an instrumental part of it all. They were the emergency asset in President Zimmer's back pocket.

As Cal and Trent entered the front door, they were greeted by a short Hispanic with an eccentric beard braided in dual strands running off his chin. Gaucho was a former Army Delta soldier and head of the squad-sized team who'd volunteered to follow Cal from SSI to The Jefferson Group.

"You take him down, boss?" Gaucho asked. By the grin on his face he obviously already knew the answer.

Cal shook his head. "Top kept trying to hug me. I hate it when he does that."

Trent punched his fellow Marine in the shoulder, knocking Cal a foot to the side.

"That's for not hugging me back," said Trent.

Cal rubbed his shoulder. "Any word from Travis?"

Travis Haden was Cal's cousin and the previous CEO of Stokes Security International. Earlier that year the former SEAL had accepted the invitation to be President Zimmer's Chief of Staff.

"Not yet," answered Gaucho.

Cal frowned. Two days before he'd gotten a call from his former platoon commander, Major Andrews. After saving each other's lives on deployment, the two Navy Cross winners had stayed in touch. Andy was the brother Cal never had. But the phone call hadn't been a "Hey how's it going?" type of call. Andy was in trouble. He hadn't said so over the phone, but Arabic shouting and gunfire in the background preceded the conversation being disconnected.

The first person Cal tried to contact after the line went dead was the man Andy had told him to call, Rich Isnard. Isnard was another former Marine who now served as the CIA station chief in Baghdad. Cal had met the rough-around-the-edges spook weeks earlier just as ISIS delivered an almost catastrophic attack against the American embassy in the heart of the Iraqi capital.

Isnard was the man responsible for recruiting Andy. While Andy wasn't yet an official member of the CIA community, he was sort of on loan to the agency, kind of a trial period to see if he'd leave his beloved Marine Corps behind. The way Isnard had explained it to Cal, it was Andy's call, but the Marine major had a knack for the intelligence business.

Unfortunately Isnard was nowhere to be found. When Cal had contacted the director of the CIA through the president, he'd been told that Isnard disappeared on occasion, sometimes for weeks at a time. It was his job to oversee covert missions throughout Iraq. Sometimes that meant going into the field.

Cal didn't like it. Something was wrong, and he was tired of waiting. Who knew where Andy was and he was sitting in Charlottesville twiddling his thumbs.

"I need to make a call," said Cal, turning down the hall and heading toward the secure War Room. Its reinforced metal door was armed with a retina scanner and the latest in security enhancements. Trent and Gaucho did not follow him.

He entered the official brain of The Jefferson Group and was surprised that no one was there. Typically there were at least two or three people manning one of the many computers arranged around the perimeter of the space. Neil Patel, their resident hacker and tech geek, was there most of each day.

Cal picked up the handset of the secure phone in the middle of the conference table and pressed the only button he ever used.

It rang once.

"Cal?" asked President Zimmer.

"Yeah. I was just checking to see if you'd heard anything about Andy."

"It's not really a good time right now, Cal."

Cal's jaw clenched. "It's been almost three days. You know what his chances look like as more time goes by."

Zimmer's voice lowered. "They're looking into it."

"What's the CIA doing to find him?"

"I have guests. Let me call you back."

Cal took a deep breath, his frustration simmering but he bit it back. "Okay. When?"

"Five minutes."

"I'll be here."

The line went dead and Cal stared at the phone. He counted down the seconds, his heart beating as his head pounded. It was just like a government agency to take its sweet time doing anything. In his time since leaving the Marine Corps, Cal's loathing for politicians and bloated bureaucracy had grown by the day. He'd experienced the lies and corruption of senators and congressmen. He'd seen billions of dollars squandered on black hole programs that the American people would never see.

All of those thoughts made him want to tear Washington down and leave it in smoking ruins. But the patriot in him knew he had to trust someone. As fate would have it, that person was a Democratic congressman turned president, Brandon Zimmer.

Their relationship had not begun well, but after saving each other's lives and surviving numerous attempts to have their careers torpedoed, the politician and Marine were close, trusting friends dedicated to the well-being of America.

The phone rang and Cal snatched it up.

"Stokes."

"Hey, sorry I had to call back. I had Secretary of Commerce in with his staff. I couldn't talk."

"No, it's my fault. I should've given you a heads up. So what do we know?"

There was a pause. Why was Zimmer hesitating?

"I just got word from the CIA."

"And?"

"It's not good."

Panic seized Cal's chest. "Just tell me. Is he dead?"

"No."

A tiny measure of relief.

"Then what?"

"It's complicated."

"Come on, it's me. Just tell me."

Another pause. Cal tried to control his breathing.

"The CIA has officially disavowed Andy."

KANDAHAR, AFGHANISTAN

The room smelled like someone had used it as a bathroom since the day the dilapidated building went up. Sour and musty like a junkie's crack house. It didn't bother Rich Isnard. He'd been to and even lived in worse places. At least he'd only be in the apartment overlooking the bustling bazaar below for the night, if that long. The cracked plastic blinds let in a filtered yellow light from the street lamps that only served to cast the room in a more depressive pallor.

Despite his repeated attempts to quit his two pack a day habit, Isnard puffed away like a man possessed. It's what he'd always done in the field. Habit, plain and simple. Like breathing.

Isnard had the hard look of a man who'd seen and done things that others might condemn. His features placed him somewhere between early thirties and mid-fifties. A forgettable face covered in salt and pepper stubble. His short hair matched his beard. To strangers, Isnard's gray eyes might look bored, but they hid the fact that the man possessed mental faculties that were always on high alert. He knew every exit in the three story complex despite only checking in an hour before. Thorough.

In his youth, he'd thrown off attempts by his overbearing mother and bitter electrician father to corral his free spirit. What do you do with a kid who's kicked out of every school in a ten mile radius?

As an only child, Isnard had ample time to observe his parents. Early on, young Richie, as his mother called him, figured out that his parents were losers. They were the type of people who complained about their circumstances instead of doing something about them. His father constantly griped about non-paying clients and freeloading employees despite the fact that he rarely got anywhere on time and almost never paid his people when he was supposed to.

His mother, the basket case, got fatter and fatter as the years creaked by, more content with bitching about the high price of milk than giving her only son anything nutritious to eat, let alone motherly love.

Rich Isnard left home at the age of seventeen after a particularly bitter fight with his father. Time had erased the reason for the argument, but the high school dropout ended up at the office of the Marine recruiter he'd met at his last high school. The young sergeant was pretty cool, even letting him bum a cigarette when they bumped into each other in the parking lot.

Much to Isnard's dismay, Sgt. Austin told him that at the time he didn't have any slots for kids without high school diplomas. He went on to explain that Isnard had to wait until he was eighteen to go to boot camp.

None of that deterred Rich Isnard. He convinced Sgt. Austin to let him sleep on his couch, promising to keep the Marine's apartment spotless in exchange for food and a place to crash. Austin agreed and set Isnard up. Isnard was true to his word. They shared the bachelor pad for two months. Time ticked by until Isnard turned eighteen. Meanwhile he took and passed the GED exam without studying.

Sgt. Austin was surprised. "How come you were failing out of school?"

Isnard grinned and replied, "I was bored."

Soon after, he got a perfect score on the Armed Services Vocational Aptitude Battery (ASVAB), which basically gave him his pick of any military occupational specialty (MOS). He'd surprised Sgt. Austin again by choosing infantry.

"Most smart kids like you want intel. You wanna be cannon fodder?" asked Sgt. Austin, who himself was an artilleryman.

Isnard shrugged. "If I'm gonna be a Marine, I'm gonna be a *real* Marine."

So two months after leaving home, Recruit Rich Isnard stood on the yellow footprints at Marine Corps Recruit Depot, Parris Island.

Despite his small stature (his initial boot camp physical measured him in at 5 feet 5 inches tall and a scrawny 120 lbs), Isnard showed his fellow recruits and the staff that he had more than enough scrap to go around. There wasn't much he couldn't do, from scoring "expert" on the rifle range and acing his academic tests, to besting his entire class on the obstacle course. He'd finally found a place where he could excel and be rewarded for it.

It was a theme that would replay wherever he went in the Marine Corps. Everyone underestimated Rich Isnard when they first met him, but it never took him long to prove his worth.

After doing four years in The Corps, Isnard used his contacts to join the CIA. By then, he'd mastered Pashtun, Chinese, Spanish and Latin (just for fun). He'd gone from pushing paper to running his own team in Iraq in under a year. He was fast-tracked by superiors who recognized his talent for the intelligence business. He read others like few could and would bend their wills when needed. If there was ever a natural spook, it was Rich Isnard.

Now, despite where he stood waiting, Rich Isnard was the CIA station chief in Baghdad, Iraq. He knew they were looking for him, but he couldn't go back. Not yet. He'd lost one of his own, his recruit, another Marine. The one thing that would always be at the foundation of Isnard's soul, a lesson learned in the first days of Marine boot camp, was that you never leave a man behind. It was a solemn promise, a vow embedded in every Marine's heart.

No. He wouldn't go back until he found out one way or another. His highly tuned mind was betting that the man he was waiting for had some insight into the whereabouts of Major "Andy" Andrews. More importantly, the contact would be the first crumb along the path of finding out why the hell the CIA had labeled Andrews a traitor.

Whether by bribery or bullet, Isnard was going to do what was needed to find the truth. He'd never failed before.

UNIVERSITY OF VIRGINIA

CHARLOTTESVILLE, VIRGINIA - 11:12AM, AUGUST 23RD

The attractive brunette with striking blue eyes walked into Little John's Deli wearing a Naval ROTC uniform. This time of year it was whites. Despite the unflattering attire, hair pulled tight in a bun and only minimal makeup, heads turned as Diane Mayer passed by. One couldn't help but look at the fourth year student who walked with an air of confidence and a genuine smile.

Cal watched the 28-year-old from the corner table, his heart beating a little faster when she smiled at him with a wave. *God, she's beautiful.*

She motioned for him to keep his seat but still leaned over the table to give him a kiss. "Hi."

"Hi," Cal replied, still amazed by the swell of emotion he felt when seeing his...well, they hadn't exactly defined their relationship yet. Diane, who'd served four years in the Navy before enrolling at U.Va., didn't like the term "boyfriend and girlfriend." While their relationship was still new, Cal was well aware of the gravitational pull drawing him to Diane.

"What did you order?" she asked, pointing down at the two sub sandwiches sitting in the middle of the well worn table.

"One Nuclear sub, extra Texas Pete, and an Italian."

They'd taken to the habit of sharing food, always halving orders. Diane grabbed a half of the Nuclear sub and took a bite. Her eyes lit up.

"I'm starving," she said with a mouthful of sandwich.

Cal smiled, grabbed the other half, and dug in.

NOT A WORD WAS SAID UNTIL THEY'D FINISHED, DIANE because she didn't stop eating, and Cal because he was enjoying the sight of a beautiful woman with an appetite she wasn't afraid to show.

"I'm going out of town tonight," he said, taking a sip of soda.

Diane stopped wiping her mouth. "Oh?"

Cal knew what she was thinking. On his last "business trip" he'd returned with a dislocated shoulder and stitches, courtesy of two weeks of sustained Ops in Iraq. Diane didn't know what he really did for a living, but he was sure she had a hunch. She wasn't stupid. Far from it, in fact.

As was his way, after the first couple dates, Cal put super hacker Neil Patel to the task of finding out about Diane Mayer. It wasn't that he didn't trust her, but he didn't like getting involved with anyone without knowing something about them. He knew the basics: family, naval service, etc.. but she'd been almost as coy as Cal when it came to telling him what she'd done in the Navy. She always said she was some kind of paper-pusher.

It hadn't taken Neil long to find out.

"She's intel," Neil had said. "Analyst. Pretty damn smart by the looks of her confidential record."

"Confidential record?" asked Cal.

Neil nodded. "Just like the special Ops guys. Looks like your girlfriend's been involved in more high level ops than you."

Neil had really gotten a kick out of that little morsel, chuckling as Cal snatched the file out of his friend's hand.

But Diane's former occupation meant more headaches for Cal. As the de facto leader of The Jefferson Group, Cal was sanctioned by President Zimmer himself. There was no one else that he answered to. If that fact was ever made public... well, it couldn't happen. He had to be careful with what he said around Diane.

"I'm not sure how long I'll be gone," said Cal, watching to see Diane's reaction.

She reached out and grabbed his hand. It was warm, comforting.

"No more stitches, okay?" she said with a grin.

Cal nodded. This was getting complicated.

* * *

Diane waved goodbye and made her way toward the Rotunda. Her next class started in ten minutes.

As she walked, thoughts filtered, still absorbing the lunch with Cal. She wasn't stupid. She knew Cal wasn't a consultant. There were thousands of consultants in the D.C. area, and Diane had met her fair share. Her time in Naval Intelligence had introduced her to the world of spy versus spy around the nation's capital.

She remembered the moment she'd checked into her first duty station and her commanding officer told her not to come to work again unless she was armed. From that day forward she had a Sig P239 no more than an arm's reach away. An expert shot, Diane had grown up in a military family. Her brothers had all served. As the baby sister, she'd gone along for the ride.

While Diane could hold her own in a military and familial establishment filled with men, she held no illusions that she could ever be a field operator. That wasn't what she wanted. Her prospects within the enlisted ranks were limited. She'd left the Navy only after applying for a ROTC scholarship and being accepted to the University of Virginia. Her dream was to be a Naval Intelligence officer. As an officer, she'd have the opportunity to have her own team, maybe even be assigned to the Defense Intelligence Agency (DIA) or Special Operations Command (SOCOM).

With an easy command of multiple languages, Diane's prospects were high. She had the experience and the brains that the Navy was looking for. Now that the Zimmer Doctrine was filtering through the federal branches, there would be an increasing need for beefed up intelligence assets. They were taking the battle to the enemy and Diane wanted to be part of it.

As luck would have it, Cal had been the proverbial wrench thrown into her well-thought-out plan. She hadn't been looking. It had just happened. But she knew that she loved him. It was the easiest of things. Under his sometimes gruff exterior lived a loving man who was loyal and kind. A born leader. She saw how he was with his friends. Guys like the enormous MSgt Trent and the crafty Gaucho deferred to Cal even when they joked with him.

Diane knew there was more to Cal than he was telling her, but she didn't push. He would tell her when the time was right.

* * *

CAL HAD SIMILAR FEELINGS AS HE WALKED AWAY FROM

lunch. He'd loved a girl once before. She'd been taken from him in the most horrific way possible: murdered right in front of him. The thought still made his heart drop, the years having done little to lessen the sting of Jessica's brutal death.

That was one of the reasons he hesitated with Diane. Besides the fact that what he did for a living was highly classified, he didn't want her to get hurt. Deep down, in a place that never saw the light of day, Cal still blamed himself for his fiancé's death. He'd replayed that night over and over again, trying to figure out what he'd done wrong. As crazy as it sounded, sometimes he felt cursed like those closest to him were the first to get punished. His parents were gone. Jess too. At least guys like his right hand man, Marine sniper Daniel Briggs, could protect themselves.

But even highly trained operators could fall on the wrong side of fate. His good friend, former Navy Corpsman Brian Ramirez, was one of them. Would Andy be next?

The thought haunted him as he made his way back to The Jefferson Group's headquarters. Cal still couldn't believe that the CIA had disavowed Andy and labeled him a traitor. Not Andy. Never.

Cal had served with his fair share of officers and Andy was the best. Unassuming, moral, and patriotic. Andy had a way, just like Daniel, of making a stressful situation better with a simple pat on the back or nod of his head. He inspired confidence in his men *and* his superiors. There was no one better to lead Marines.

That's why the thought of Andy being a traitor was so ludicrous. *No way*.

Hopefully he'd have some answers soon. His team should be waiting. He had to talk to them first, then it was on to Washington. If the president didn't have the answers, Cal would find them some other way.

HELMAND PROVINCE, AFGHANISTAN

6:03AM AFT, AUGUST 24TH

They had a new game now. Instead of delivering severed body parts to his cell, a trio of guards would come into the room, blindfold him, unhook his manacles from the wall, attach a cold metal collar to his neck, and drag him out like a dog. They even made barking sounds and tried to trip him like kids do.

Once outside they would parade him around, jabbering on about what a good dog he was, apparently not knowing that he could understand every word. They never hit him. It was just like taking a dog for a walk. Andy didn't have a clue what they were doing.

As well as he could estimate, they did this every hour or two. He didn't have his watch so he couldn't be sure, but it felt like hour-long intervals. He'd started the habit of counting down the seconds. Tedious, but what else was he going to do?

They kept it up throughout the night, killing any chance of getting sleep.

They were either toying with him or wearing him down in the most obscure way he'd ever experienced. He'd had briefings on captivity and torture. He knew what to expect. But this wasn't it. There had to be a reason...

He'd just dozed off when the cell door creaked open and the guards streamed in. Gone were the playful smirks, replaced by grim determination. No one said a word as they ran through the practiced routine, leading him out of the structure into the still morning air.

Andy's ears strained to hear anything that would give away his captors' intent, but none came. One of them pushed him to the ground, and in broken English, said "Sit."

He sat, and waited. It didn't take long.

Soon he heard the sound of vehicles approaching. He couldn't tell, but he estimated between five and ten. Car doors opened and shut and he could just make out the muffled conversations coming from the passengers. They were talking about him.

In Pashtun one of the men said, "Stand him up."

Andy's heart beat faster as strong hands grabbed him under his arms and hoisted him to his feet.

"Tell me why you've come to my country," the same voice said again, still in Pashtun.

Andy ignored the question. They didn't need to know that he understood the language. Let them think that he was just another no name contractor who didn't speak a lick of the local dialect.

Again in Pashtun, the man said, "Come now, Major Andrews. I know that you speak my language. Do not be rude. Please answer my question."

While it didn't necessarily surprise him, it did add to his worry. If they knew who he was, it was only a matter of time before they knew he was working for the CIA. And if they knew that...

"I asked you a question, Major." The man's voice sounded cultured, unlike the men who'd guarded him since his capture.

"I'm in Afghanistan on a humanitarian mission with White Dove International." It was his official cover and he'd actually gone through the steps of being hired by the non-profit as a sort of ambassador for the region. His job with White Dove was to find Afghan communities in need of assistance and organize the shipment and distribution of aid. It gave him the ability to travel wherever and whenever he needed.

"And please tell me, Major, does White Dove International know that you also work for the Central Intelligence Agency?" The man had switched to near flawless English, his accent faint.

"I don't know what you're talking about. I am a former Marine who..."

"According to my sources you are an anomaly, Major. Still listed as an active duty Marine Corps officer, you have apparently done work for the CIA for close to six months. Is this not true?"

"It is not."

"It would be better if we could be honest with each other, Major. There are some in my country who would like to see you drawn and quartered on national television. Is that what you want?"

"Call White Dove. Ask them who I am. They'll tell you..."

The man snapped his fingers and the sound produced an immediate result. The butt of a rifle slammed into Andy's abdomen, blasting the air from his lungs. He resisted the urge to kneel, waiting for his body to naturally regain its ability to breath.

"Despite what you might think, we Afghans are a civilized culture. Our people established this community centuries before your country was even a wisp of a thought. There have been many nations which have come and gone in that time. You Americans are only the most recent. I am sure that because of your Marine background you are well aware of our history, our ability to outlast even the most brutal invaders. Let us bring that same concept into our current situation. I am a patient man, Major, but my patience has limits. You either cooperate with us now, or your entire operation will become public knowledge."

Andy's stomach clenched. There was no way they knew... unless someone within the CIA had tipped them off.

The man continued. "So while I applaud your noble intentions and understand that you will fight us until the last breath escapes your lips, I am equally sure that you have no idea what the repercussions would be should you continue your mission."

Andy had no idea what the man was talking about. He'd flown into Helmand on a hunch, a simple investigative trip. What swarm of hornets had he uncovered?

"I will leave you with one final thought, Major, a gift really. What you might not know is that steps have already been taken by your country to distance itself from you."

"What are you talking about?" The last he'd heard he was in perfect standing with the CIA. Hell, he was still the new guy. No one knew him.

The man chuckled. "Have you ever heard the term *disavowed*, Major?"

Andy's throat seized.

"I had to look the word up. According to your English dictionary, the term disavowed means to refuse responsibility for something or someone, or to deny its existence. That is what your CIA has done to you, Major. To them you no longer exist. You are a figment of your own imagination. A ghost. A traitor."

Andy shook his head. It couldn't be. Nothing he'd done could be construed that way. He was a Marine for God's sake. Maybe this man was lying. Maybe he...

All of a sudden the nagging recognition that had been tapping away in his subconscious coalesced into clarity. He knew who the man was.

"I will give you the day to think about it, Major. Cooperate with us and your death will be swift. A warrior's death. Deny my request and...well, we Afghanis do have creative ways of seeing men suffer. The media will love the story of a Marine on loan to the CIA conducting an unsanctioned operation inside Afghanistan... Get some sleep today. You will not be bothered. I will be back tomorrow morning. Good day, Major."

Andy heard the opening and closing of car doors. Not rusted pickups or late model sedans. The heavy thud of armored SUVs. More proof that the man was who Andy suspected.

As they dragged him back to his cell, Andy tried to find a silver lining in his predicament. He searched for a way out, a reason why his own government was turning its back on him. None came. If this man had taken the time to see him, Major Andrews had tripped on something much larger than he'd suspected. But what could it be?

THE WHITE HOUSE

He ran a hand through his dirty blond hair, a yawn accompanying the gesture. It had been a very long day. As the Chief of Staff to the President of The United States of America, Travis Haden rarely left the office before midnight. There was simply too much to do. If it wasn't a raging policy battle, it was another imminent threat from one of the many crazies around the world.

The former SEAL was used to stress. While getting his trident had been tough, and leading a global security company like SSI had been challenging, his new role eclipsed them both by far. Some days, he wished he was getting shot at again instead of having bundles and bundles of reports and requests delivered daily. The level of hypocrisy alone was enough to send him running. The warrior in him growled, but the loyal public servant calmed the unease by recognizing the importance of his contribution.

President Zimmer needed him. It still amazed Travis to

think of all they'd accomplished in less than a year. When he'd asked Travis to join him in Washington, Zimmer had made two requests. "Help me clean up my cabinet." That was the easy part. Most of those people had known the reshuffling was coming.

The second request was less defined, more strategic, and yet, the reason Travis had said yes to the new position.

"Help me be a good president," Zimmer had said.

While the request might've seemed simple to others, Travis understood the breadth of what the president wanted. Zimmer wasn't just worried about his legacy, he wanted to do it right. He wanted to be a fair leader worthy of the office. That meant surrounding himself with people like Travis and the Chairman of the Joint Chiefs, General McMillan, USMC, men and women whose sole purpose in life was to do the right thing, even if it meant challenging their boss's point of view.

Travis felt like they were succeeding. The whole Zimmer Doctrine idea was gaining steam. International allies rallied to the president's call. Terrorists were running scared, pursued by eager military veterans and their active duty brethren. They'd even made some headway with the economy.

Yeah, things were going in the right direction, but there was still so much to do.

That brought him to this latest problem. *Andy*.

He'd been introduced to the Marine years before, when his cousin Cal had brought the young officer home after returning from Iraq. The guy was sharp, a born leader. Travis had met all manner of men in his years in the military and with SSI. He knew honest men, men with the morals of patriotic warriors. Andy was one of those guys.

Or so he'd thought.

Earlier in the day, he and the president met with the CIA director, his deputy director of National Clandestine Service (NCS) and the CIA's inspector general.

Travis knew the director, but had never met the other two. The president said he'd only met them in passing.

They'd come at the president's request, more of a favor than an official tasking. The picture they painted of Major Andrews contrasted harshly with the image Travis had of the lost Marine.

"Mr. President, we have overwhelming proof, including video, phone transcripts and witnesses that prove Major Andrews' guilt," explained the inspector general. His voice was nasally and pompous. "We've also uncovered at least five overseas accounts containing just under thirty million dollars, all held by known aliases of Major Andrews."

"And what exactly are you saying he's guilty of, gentlemen?" asked the president, his eyes boring into the almost flippant inspector general.

The director saw the simmering anger in the president's eyes and cut in before the Inspector General could respond.

"Sir, we believe Major Andrews is part of a larger conspiracy to discredit the United States and embezzle millions of dollars earmarked for aid projects in the Middle East."

They'd shown them the files, the videos, the proof that Andy was what they were accusing him of being: a traitor. Neither man wanted to believe it, but the deck seemed insurmountably stacked against the Marine.

And yet, something nagged at the edges of Travis's vision. It all seemed too tight, too perfect. Ask any cop on the street or FBI agent in the field, an investigation was rarely this cut and dried.

The other thing that bothered Travis was the deputy

director. Sitting there with his perfectly manicured fingernails and Savile Row suit, the man looked more like a person heading an international luxury brand than leading the most powerful clandestine service in the world. The man's silence did little to ease Travis's suspicions.

So instead of going home and facing Cal, who had texted every thirty minutes for an update, Travis sat at his desk and conducted his own investigation. Luckily the Secret Service owed him a few favors, and it only took one phone call to get their file on the CIA's Deputy Director NCS, Kingsley Coles.

A Harvard grad, Coles had done a stint in the Army after college. Intelligence. After fulfilling his four year commitment, he'd gone back to Harvard for his Juris Doctor, then spent thirteen years in environmental law, suing large corporations who were killing Mother Earth. Coles had become a very wealthy man.

Strangely enough, he'd entered public service on some sort of grant funded by the government in the wake of 9-11. Coles left private practice, even giving up his position as partner to serve his country. He'd done a year stint with the State Department then made his way to the CIA.

It didn't look like the guy had any field experience. That would most certainly have precluded Coles from attaining his current position ten years before; however Zimmer's predecessor, after repeated CIA snafus, ushered in a slew of political appointees to positions formerly held by CIA lifers.

It looked like Coles was one of those guys. Someone who'd been brought in to clean house, to polish up the image of the American spy network. Travis shook his head. Sure there were plenty of subpar employees in the CIA just like any government entity, but putting an attorney in the spot rightfully reserved for a field veteran was just wrong.

Beyond that, something didn't feel right about the guy. It

wasn't anything Travis could put his finger on, but his senses were tingling.

Either way, that would have to wait until morning. Right now he had to call Cal and give him the bad news. It wasn't looking good for Andy.

ARLINGTON, VIRGINIA

12:52AM, AUGUST 24TH

The veins in Cal's hand bulged as he gripped the phone. His chest heaved like a bull waiting to go into a matador's ring. He closed his eyes as he listened, trying to focus on steadying his breathing. His temper howled inside demanding to be unleashed.

"You know that's impossible, Trav," Cal managed to say into the phone, his voice flat, emotionless.

"I know, but until we have evidence to support Andy, there's not much we can do."

"Don't tell me that. I couldn't care less about the evidence. We need to get Andy back. Not tomorrow. Now."

"Look, if the president goes against the CIA it would ruin the inroads we've made. I think..."

"So you're saying I should sit here and wait until my email dings and I get the video with Andy's head dangling from some terrorist's hand?"

"That's not what I'm saying, Cal. Unofficially, of course,

the president agrees with you. But we need to be careful. Have you heard from Isnard?"

"No. He's gone deep somewhere. Every line we've put out there has yet to get a bite."

"I'm sure he'll call as soon as he has something," said Travis.

"Yeah. I sure hope so."

* * *

HELMAND PROVINCE, AFGHANISTAN - 8:37AM AFT, AUGUST 24TH

The white delivery truck pulled up the long drive, escorted by two pickup trucks and the usual complement of gunmen. You didn't go anywhere in Helmand without security, least of all if you had something of value in your possession. Food was on the top of that list.

Quraish gazed down from his perch atop one of the squat buildings of the village. He sat in the best place to view the steep approach of the road below. It was early for a delivery, but at least they might have something better than the stale bread and moldy cheese they'd been given at sunup. One of the others had told him that supplies were running low. Quraish's belly rumbled at the thought.

Someone in the larger village below had undoubtedly checked the convoy and passed it through. This was the innermost of three security rings. Besides, this side of the river was protected by a local warlord who ensured its safety. No one set foot inside the warlord's lands without permission.

Quraish clicked his radio twice then spoke into it. "Food delivery coming up from the village."

Whoever was on the other end mumbled something Quraish couldn't understand. He replaced the radio on the short wall and continued to watch the small caravan as it moved closer. Still bored, Quraish's only hope was that there would be some food left by the time his shift was over.

* * *

THE THREE VEHICLES PULLED TO A STOP IN FRONT OF THE main building. Although larger than the others, the home was missing a quarter of its roof courtesy of an American mortar.

A five man contingent from the group assigned to defend the small outpost walked out to meet the delivery. Like their friend on the roof, their stomachs growled at the thought of food.

The men in the beds of the pickups stayed where they were as three men piled out of the delivery truck. One approached the defenders and the other two moved to the rear of the vehicle.

"Good morning, brothers," said the lone man who approached, arms spread wide in greeting. His face was covered with a dust crusted black scarf. He wore a rust colored pakol on his head, the traditional Afghan round-topped cap worn by many in the rural region. Even the man's eyes were shielded with dark sunglasses rimmed with brown dirt. "Where should I have my men put your shipment?"

"Have them take it over there," one of the five said, pointing to the building they'd come out of. "What did you bring today?"

The delivery man pulled down his scarf revealing a yellow smile. He rubbed his hands together.

"Many fine surprises, my friend. Many fine. Tell me, how many men do you have so that I might leave enough extras? Nothing you need to tell your commander about. I know how it is on duty."

The five men looked at each other, one finally answering. "There are ten, but one is an old man with no teeth."

The delivery man smiled wide and clapped his hands once. "Good! Then I have brought enough. No treat is too good for our fine warriors." He put up a finger as if to say, "Wait here."

The man disappeared behind the truck and came out a moment later cradling something wrapped in a white linen veil. The smile hadn't left his face.

"What is it?" asked one of the men, who now numbered seven. The rest nodded in anticipation.

With a flourish, the delivery man whipped the linen away revealing a Russian-made PKM medium machine gun. On instinct, the seven men went for their weapons, but hesitated when the armed man standing in front of them whistled to get their attention. He motioned with his head back over his shoulder.

The outpost security guards looked where he was pointing and saw the rest of the caravan pointing their guns straight at them. It only took a second for them to realize they were outgunned.

"Now, if you will be kind and lower your weapons, I promise that we are not here to harm you," said the delivery man.

"How do we know you won't kill us as soon as we do what you say?" one of the guards dared to ask.

The delivery man laughed. "Do you think we would be here if we didn't have your master's permission? This is all part of the plan. We'll even leave you the food in the back of the truck. No harm, eh?"

"Then what do you want?"

"First, I want you to put your weapons on the ground. Then I want to talk to whoever is in charge."

Six of the guards looked to a seventh. He shook his head in disgust.

"It looks like you are in charge," the delivery man said to the seventh. "Let's step over there while they unload the truck."

The two men moved away from the others and stopped next to a gray bricked well.

"Where is the American?" asked the delivery man. His smile was gone.

"I don't know what..."

"I could easily kill you now and ask one of your underlings. You have two seconds to decide. One..."

The seventh man put up his hands. "In that building." He pointed down the row to the smallest structure of the bunch.

The delivery man nodded. "Take me."

* * *

ANDY'S EYES SNAPPED TO THE DOOR. HE'D HEARD THE crunch of tires and the slamming of car doors. They were back for him.

The wooden portal creaked open and one of the guards walked in with his hands raised, followed immediately by a shorter man wearing sunglasses and carrying an impressive machine gun.

"Get up," ordered the armed man.

Andy lifted his bound hands to show him that he couldn't.

"Where are the keys?" the man asked.

"In my pocket," said the guard.

"Well take them out and unlock him, you fool."

The guard did as instructed, inserted the skeleton key and took the heavy chains off of Andy.

"Now sit down and put them on yourself."

The guard nodded and set both cuffs on his wrists. He glared at the second man as Andy backed away cautiously. He didn't have a clue what was going on. Possibly some sort of power struggle. Kidnapping and extortion were big business in Afghanistan. It looked like he'd just been snatched by another faction. Confirmation came when the stranger tossed him a pair of handcuffs.

"Put them on."

Andy complied.

"Now open the door and walk outside."

Andy led the way out of the room, maintaining a safe distance from the weapon that had yet to be lowered.

"Walk to the delivery truck," his new captor ordered. "Get in the front."

Andy nodded, keeping his head lowered, even as his eyes darted back and forth. There were men he recognized, the guards, unloading food from the back of a white delivery truck. Other men sitting in the beds of smaller pickups watched, weapons trained.

This could go either way. Careful not to get in the path of his former guards who threw hateful glares his way, Andy climbed in the passenger side of the cab. The smell of stale cigarettes greeted him as he sat back and waited for the next leg of his journey.

* * *

ONCE ALL THE FOOD WAS DEPOSITED NEXT TO THEIR weapons, the delivery man gathered the outpost guards together.

"As I told you when I arrived, I am here at the bidding of someone much more important than any one of us. That puts you in a dilemma. If your boss finds out that you let the prisoner out..." He shook his head, confirming the implication.

"So what do we do?" asked one of the guards, panic in his

bloodshot eyes.

The delivery man nodded slowly, thinking. Then he said, "I secured your leader in the same cell where you held your former prisoner. I would suggest that if you want to relieve yourself of the burden of blame, do with him what you like. After all, was it not *his* responsibility to secure this outpost? Perhaps retell the story of how *he* orchestrated the prisoner's escape, how he failed to lift a finger."

The six remaining guards nodded. They all knew what would happen if the blame lay in their hands.

"I think you know what you must do, brothers. Good luck."

The delivery man turned and headed back to his truck, the engines of the pickup trucks revving in preparation for their departure.

"How do you know we will not tell the truth?" asked another guard.

The delivery man shrugged. "If that is your wish, may Allah grant you a swift death." He handed the PKM to one of his men and climbed into the driver's seat. "Farewell friends. Enjoy the food. The dates are especially delicious."

All six guards stood in muted shock and watched the caravan make its way out of the outpost. As soon as the sound of tire on gravel faded down the hill, all six men turned and headed to the prisoner's cell.

* * *

ANDY DIDN'T SAY A WORD AS THE CONVOY CLEARED THE last building and rumbled onto the dirt road heading down a steep hill. It was the first chance he'd had to see the surrounding area. They were heading into a broad valley, homes dotting the landscape below.

Once they'd made it half a mile from his former prison,

the delivery man pulled out an Afghan cigarette and lit it with a cheap lighter. He took a deep pull, held it, then let the gray plume out through the side of his mouth.

Without turning to look at Andy he said, "I'll tell you what, they sure make Marines uglier than when I went through Parris Island."

It took Andy a moment to realize the guy had said it in English and that he now recognized the voice. He turned his head as the driver took off the sunglasses and threw him a wink.

"Rich," Andy breathed, relief flooding his body. The spook was the last person he was expecting to see. He hadn't seen Isnard since passing through Baghdad, which seemed like ages ago.

Rich Isnard smiled and tossed Andy a set of keys. "Take your handcuffs off and grab the gun under your seat." He pointed to the road ahead. "We're going to have company."

Andy shifted his gaze and saw what Isnard was talking about. There was a much larger convoy of vehicles coming their way. He knew it was the men behind his capture.

"With just a little bit of luck we'll let them fly by and it might buy us some time before they talk to the boys back there."

"That's your plan?" asked Andy, reaching under the seat and feeling the familiar touch of a rifle stock.

"Hey, man, I put this little rescue op together on the fly. Semper Gumby, right?"

Isnard was grinning like a teenager who'd just gotten to third base with the captain of the cheerleading squad. Something about his smile reminded Andy of another Marine who was known for his bold charge into the maw of the enemy: Cal Stokes. With any luck, they'd survive the day and Andy might have a chance to tell his old friend what he'd discovered.

HELMAND PROVINCE, AFGHANISTAN

9:17AM AFT, AUGUST 24TH

The smaller convoy of three eased off the road to allow the oncoming vehicles to pass. There were two humvees in the lead, one sporting a .50 caliber mounted machine gun, the second armed with a Mark-19 grenade launcher. Made in America.

Next came the large black SUVs, their windows an impenetrable black. There were ten, then another three humvees bringing up the rear.

Isnard whistled.

"That's a lot of firepower."

Andy half expected the opposing force to stop and take them out.

"Figures."

Isnard turned to look at him. "What do you know? I couldn't get confirmation on who was holding you. All they told me was that it was someone high up. I pulled every damned string I could just to get that much."

Andy told him. Isnard's face hardened.

"Are you sure?" he asked.

Andy nodded. "I recognized his voice."

Isnard put the truck in drive and pulled out onto the road, his lips tight in concentration.

"There's a phone in the glove box. Grab it."

Andy opened the compartment, moved aside extra packs of cigarettes and found a scuffed gray cell phone. He held it out for Isnard. Isnard shook his head.

"If what you're telling is true, we've probably got one call with that thing."

"It's not encrypted?"

"I couldn't get my hands on anything better in time."

"Wait. Does the Agency know you're out here?"

Isnard made a face. "Not exactly."

Andy didn't understand. He'd assumed that the CIA ordered Isnard to find him. Now that he had a second to think about it, he realized it was strange that the Baghdad station chief was in Afghanistan.

"Tell me what I missed."

Isnard told him what he knew, which wasn't much. The most important part being that Major Andrews was now disavowed by the employer who'd sent him into Afghanistan. For some reason Andy wasn't surprised. He started laughing.

Isnard looked at him with a raised eyebrow. "You want to tell me what's so funny? Last time I checked we're in this thing neck deep, Marine."

Andy threw his hands up. "You know, everyone told me to stay away from the CIA, but I didn't listen. I should be XO of a battalion right now. Instead, you're telling me that on my very first operation for the CIA, I get captured, you save me like a knight in shining armor, AND I've been disowned? I'm sorry, but all I can think to do is laugh."

Isnard chuckled. "You're right. It's like a really crappy

movie, right? The kind you can't keep watching because you know it's fake."

Andy's laughing died down.

"How are we getting out of here?"

Isnard gave him a thin smile. "I hadn't quite figured that out yet. Truth be told, I gave my rescue operation a thirty-percent chance of success. On top of that, my boss is pissed with me. I've been dodging his calls since I left Baghdad. He's not stupid. He probably knows what I've been up to and for all I know I've been disavowed too."

Both men chuckled at that. It really was too much to think about. There they were, in the middle of enemy territory, and they couldn't trust their own government to save them.

"So who do we call?" asked Andy, pointing to the cell phone.

Isnard smiled. "We need someone who's just nuts enough to come get us."

Andy returned the smile when he realized to whom Isnard was referring. "Cal Stokes."

* * *

ARLINGTON, VIRGINIA - 1:53AM, AUGUST 24TH

The buzzing from the cell phone shook Cal from his thoughts. He'd been lying in bed for almost an hour, replaying the last conversation with Travis. Things looked bleak and he could feel Andy's chances dwindling as the minutes ticked by.

He picked up the phone from the bedside table and looked at the screen. The caller ID displayed *UNKNOWN* in bold. Cal didn't get a lot of calls and the unidentified ones were rarer still.

Curious, Cal answered the call.

"Hello?"

"Yeah, I was told that if I wanted a good time I should call this number?"

Cal bolted upright. It was Andy. He was being vague for a reason. Probably a nonsecure phone. He played along.

"Yeah. Depends on what you need." Cal's heart pounded as he waited for any hint of where his friend was.

"We kinda got in a little thing with some old friends and we might need a ride home."

"That can be arranged. Where?"

"I was thinking we could meet at the same place you got cozy with Jiffy John."

It took Cal a moment to realize what Andy was alluding to. On one of their trips back from overseas deployment, Cal caught a mean case of the runs. He'd spent their entire layover in Kandahar in a port-a-potty. After that, Andy always said he had a thing for Jiffy John, the American brand of portable bathrooms.

"Yeah, I remember."

"Good. I'm not sure when we'll be there, but keep your phone on when you get in. Oh, and bring some friends."

"You got it. Hey, are you okay?"

There was a pause from Andy's end, then he replied. "I'm a lot better than I was an hour ago. I've even got a mutual friend driving. He said he'd be happy to give you another tour when you get here."

Cal heard honking in the background.

"I'll see you soon," said Cal.

"Right. Gotta go."

The line went dead and Cal stared at his phone. At least Andy was safe for the moment. He now knew his friend was with Rich Isnard. The comment about the tour referred to when Cal had first met the wily spook. He'd taken Cal on a walking tour of the U.S. Embassy in Baghdad, not letting on until later that he was friends with Andy.

Getting into Afghanistan wouldn't be a problem. The hard part would be doing it without anyone knowing. Based on what Travis had told him, the CIA was high on the list of suspects in Andy's disappearance. Keeping a rescue operation off their radar would be almost impossible. They had assets everywhere.

Cal stood and cracked his neck from side to side. Impossible or not, at least he could do something about it now.

HELMAND PROVINCE, AFGHANISTAN

9:26AM AFT, AUGUST 24TH

The goat herder and his charges took their time crossing the road. There had to be hundreds of scrawny goats meandering over the dust and gravel strip. Isnard hardly let off the horn. The sound did little to move the procession. The hunched Afghan didn't even look up.

After what seemed like ages, the last goats ambled past. The lead pickup truck gunned its engine and started moving. No sooner had it gone fifty yards that the vehicle and the five men inside blew sky high. Unlike the movies, there was no fireball, just twisted metal and body parts flying.

Isnard didn't let off the gas, the delivery truck thumping along the debris-strewn road even as half their security team landed twenty feet away.

"What the hell was that?" asked Andy, trying to look in the side mirror. The mirror had been destroyed long before, so he couldn't see a thing.

"The convoy's back," said Isnard, pointing with his thumb

over his shoulder. He swerved their lumbering target left and right, reminding Andy of his basic training and hours of dodging left and right, saying "I'm up, they see me, I'm down," as his squad maneuvered down the live fire range. But the hulk of a truck they were riding in couldn't take cover. There was no ducking. Instead the spook jockeyed the wheel erratically, trying to make them a harder target to hit.

There was an explosion three car lengths ahead. They drove straight through the plume of dust. Another two explosions on their left, just where they'd been a split second before.

Andy could hear the rear security team answering with an endless rattle of machine gun fire. It was probably the only thing giving them time.

The PKM Isnard had was too cumbersome to hold and fire out the window, so Andy used the battered rifle instead. He couldn't see much when he stuck his head out. Any shot he took might hit their own escort in the second pickup truck.

Just as he pulled his head back in the cab, a shadow passed overhead followed by the telltale sound of aircraft engines and propellers. Andy knew the sound instinctively: attack helicopter. He got confirmation a moment later as he watched a Marine Corps AH-1Z Viper, the recent replacement for the AH-1W Super Cobra, bank left and over and head back toward the road.

Loaded with ample 20mm ammunition for its M197 3-barreled Gatling cannons and a full compliment of 70mm APKWS II rockets, Andy knew from experience that their humble two-vehicle convoy was no match should the helicopter engage. There wasn't a chance in hell he was going to shoot at fellow Marines, so instead he just watched as the helicopter turned and followed the delivery truck's path.

* * *

"You want me to take them out with the gun or the rockets, Skipper?" asked 1ˢᵗ Lt. Adam "Digger" Reeve, USMCR. He had a clear shot of the white delivery truck and the pickup behind it.

"Let's see if your aim is any better than it was two days ago, Digger. Go with the cannon," replied Major Donald "Brickhouse" Barricado, USMC.

"Roger that, Skipper," said Digger, taking his time lining up a perfect shot. It was a little game they played. See how few shots it took to take down a target. Any idiot could do it with a heat-seeker. But the skipper was old school, a mustang who loved to extol the virtues of World War II era Marines flying their Wildcats over the Pacific, engaging the enemy with crude machine guns. One of his favorite things to do was explain how a pilot used to have to "walk" rounds into a target instead of the infinitely easier point and click of the modern age weaponry.

While some of the other squadron gunners groaned at the tales, Digger listened and practiced. He was getting to where it only took the briefest burst from the cannon to destroy lightly armored vehicles. He'd even pierced an engine block a couple weeks earlier, allowing the troops on the ground to capture the Taliban outlaws driving the small sedan.

But their orders were not to disable. This was supposed be a kill shot. Brief and painless. Well, at least for him.

Satisfied that he had a handle on the delivery truck's movement, Digger reached for the trigger that would send a stream of 20mm rounds downrange, delivering the faceless enemy to hell in a heartbeat.

"Hold one, Digger," said the skipper.

Digger exhaled in frustration. "Sir?"

"We're getting an IFF signal from that truck." The pilot's voice was incredulous.

"A transponder?" asked Digger. Only aircraft carried the IFF (identification friend or foe) transponder that allowed military aircraft to ID each other. But not just anyone could use them. The U.S. military, NATO and their allies, used an encrypted system that had to be fed secure validations daily in order to be considered legit. "Is it one of ours?"

"Apparently."

"You think some jihadi got their hands on one of ours?"

"I don't see how they could. Call it in will you?"

"Yes, sir."

* * *

A MOMENT EARLIER, ISNARD HAD REACHED UNDER HIS SEAT and fiddled with something. "That should give us a breather."

The helicopter was still shadowing them, but apparently whatever the spook had done was giving the pilot and his gunner pause.

"What did you do?" asked Andy.

"On the off chance that some flyboy thought we were a juicy target, I brought along my lucky transponder so they'd know we're not the bad guys."

"But if the real bad guys are controlling them, what's to stop them? You know they'll override anything we do."

Isnard grinned. "Stick your hand all the way under your seat. I brought something else, just in case."

* * *

"SIR, HIGHER SAYS TO ENGAGE."

Maj. Barricado easily kept pace with the two-vehicle

convoy. Something didn't feel right. He'd engaged countless insurgents over multiple tours in Afghanistan and Iraq. It didn't matter if they were on the run or not, if they could see you, they fired at you, even if you were a speck on the horizon. It was human nature. Try to shoot down the thing in the sky before it blows you to bits.

But this target wasn't firing at him. And then there was the thing with the transponder. Unless the driver and his pal had paid a king's ransom for U.S. military equipment earlier that day...

"I'm moving in for a closer look," he announced, already having pushed his aircraft's nose forward.

"You sure, Skipper? We've got the go-ahead."

Maj. Barricado ignored his co-pilot. He wanted to see this for himself.

* * *

ANDY SHOOK HIS HEAD WHEN HE HELD UP WHAT HE'D found wedged behind a fire extinguisher under his seat.

"You're kidding, right?"

Isnard shrugged, a grin playing at the corner of his mouth. "Didn't you learn the KISS rule at OCS, Major Andrews? Besides, I never leave home without it."

Despite the situation, Andy chuckled and stuck the object out the window with both hands.

* * *

"ARE YOU SEEING THIS?" ASKED MAJ. BARRICADO.

"I'll be damned."

Now being held up just outside the passenger side door, fluttering from the breeze but unmistakable to the career

Marine, was a red flag with yellow fringe, the United States Marine Corps's Eagle, Globe and Anchor prominently displayed in gold in the center. Next to it was a man's face. Dirty and gaunt, but recognizable enough to see that the man wasn't of Arabic descent.

It took a moment for Barricado to speak.

"Tell higher we had an engine malfunction," he said as he pulled the aircraft violently to the right, as if overcorrecting or dodging something he'd just seen in the air.

"Skipper?"

"Just do it, Digger. Oh, and why don't you lob a couple rockets between those two convoys."

It must have finally dawned on his sometimes naive co-pilot what was happening, because a moment later Major "Brickhouse" Barricado watched as four rockets leapt from their positions and screamed to their destination. "Semper Fi, boys."

Without waiting to see the outcome, trusting Digger's gunnery skills, Barricado banked right and headed for home.

* * *

ANDY HELD HIS BREATH AS THE ROCKETS LEFT THE MARINE attack helicopter and blazed toward their mark. *Two, one...*

The projectiles didn't follow the delivery truck. He heard the explosions behind them and said a quick thanks to whoever the Marine aviators were. Maybe some day he would find them and buy them a beer. Hell, he'd buy them a damn brewery for what they'd done.

"Looks like our friends stopped," Isnard announced, grabbing another cigarette from his endless supply. The Marine aviators had stopped the pursuing vehicles cold.

"You're one crazy bastard, you know that?" said Andy. He

was smiling, but a sheen of moisture threatened to turn into tears.

"Don't thank me yet, jarhead. I'm sure that won't be the last of it."

As they reached the road that would take them away from the protected village cluster, Andy wondered how many lives he had left, and if he would get to see Cal in Kandahar.

THE WHITE HOUSE

The president was waiting in a blue bathrobe and Travis was wearing PT gear when Cal entered the residence. Their conversation stopped when the Marine walked in.

"Thanks for seeing me," said Cal, still not sure what he was going to tell his friends. On one hand he trusted them both without question. On the other, his buddy Brandon was the President of The United States and Cal's cousin was the president's chief of staff. Anything they knew would be scrutinized. It was one hell of a position to be in considering the level of responsibility and the parties they had to keep happy. What Cal had in mind would ruffle more than a few feathers. Part of him had decided to leave without saying a word, but Daniel had convinced him otherwise.

"It sounded urgent," Zimmer offered, his look sharp despite the early morning wakeup call and the bags under his eyes.

"It is." Cal took a seat in the armchair across from the president. "I heard from Andy."

Both Zimmer and Travis sat up straighter. Zimmer spoke first. "Where is he?"

Cal debated holding back the whole truth. What if the information got back to the CIA? Who knew what those bastards were hiding? *Screw it.*

"He's still in Afghanistan and it looks like he's with Rich Isnard."

The president and Travis looked at each other, a silent thought passing between them.

"What?" asked Cal.

The president leaned forward. "Right after you called, I got an update from the CIA."

A chill ran up Cal's spine. Was he too late?

"What did they say?"

"They've placed Isnard on administrative leave, indefinitely."

"What did they say he did?"

Another look passed between the president and his chief of staff. Travis answered this time.

"Apparently Afghan forces were in pursuit of a person of interest and had called in Marine close air support. The Marines were given the go-ahead to take out the target. It didn't go exactly as planned, and somewhere in the mix an IFF transponder was used that was traced back to Isnard."

"I don't get it. What does this have to do with Isnard?"

"As it was explained to us, Isnard always lugs this transponder around when he's in the field. His boss said it wasn't sanctioned by the Agency, but Isnard's a pretty convincing guy. Gets most anything he wants. Anyway, he takes it in the field just in case one of our birds decides to tag his incognito mode of transport. You know the kinds of people he deals with. I don't blame him for protecting his butt."

"I still don't understand why the CIA is going after him for this," said Cal.

Travis exhaled. "As part of our agreement with the Afghan government, our forces support their forces. Instead of blowing up the bad guys, our Marine Viper had some kind of malfunction and almost destroyed the Afghan convoy. The Afghans think it's bullshit, some kind of conspiracy. They're pissed and want to know who's responsible."

"Let me guess, the Marine pilot's been grounded too."

Travis shrugged. "Pending the investigation, yes."

The story sounded like a convoluted mess. As Cal digested the news, a thought dawned on him. What if the Afghan army was involved in Andy's kidnapping?

As if reading his mind, Zimmer said, "Someone's playing games here and I'm afraid Isnard and Andy are stuck in the middle."

"What is the CIA doing about it?" asked Cal.

"They're giving me a briefing at nine with a detailed action plan. You're welcome to listen in, remotely, of course."

Cal shook his head. "I can't, but you can fill me in." He stood up from his chair. "I've gotta go."

"Wait, where are you going?" asked Zimmer, rising from his seat.

"Afghanistan."

"I don't think that's a good idea, Cal."

The president grabbed Cal by the arm. Cal looked back.

"Unlike the CIA, I'm not one to leave my friends behind."

Zimmer let go of Cal's arm and nodded.

"Officially, I should tell you to wait and let..."

Cal's eyes hardened. "You sanctioned The Jefferson Group to..."

Zimmer put up a hand. "Let me finish. I was going to say that as the president I should let the CIA do their job."

"And?"

Zimmer's eyes softened. "As your boss and as a friend, I wanted to say good luck and be careful. I'm afraid you won't know who to trust when you get there." The two men stared at each other for a moment, and Cal finally nodded.

"Thanks."

"I know I don't have to tell you that if you go, you and whomever you take with you are on your own. I can't officially know about this."

Cal grinned. "Don't worry, Mr. President, we'll be in and out before you can say *Chesty Puller at the Chosin*."

CHARLOTTESVILLE-ALBEMARLE AIRPORT

CHARLOTTESVILLE, VIRGINIA - 5:57AM, AUGUST 24TH

It took all his willpower for Cal not to tap his foot or punch a wall. He should've been on his way to Afghanistan, but he'd hopped a flight from D.C. to Charlottesville on the suggestion of The Jefferson Group's CEO, Jonas Layton. It took more than a little urging for Cal to delay his journey. *This better be good*, he thought for maybe the hundredth time.

Daniel was inside the small terminal waiting for the coffee shop to open. That left Cal on the edge of the tarmac, waiting. It wasn't a skill he was particularly good at as evidenced by the repeated glances at his watch and iPhone.

Jonas had called ahead, instructing the airport staff to escort Cal and Daniel to a spot near a newly renovated private hangar. It was empty and the door locked.

A cool breeze blew across the runway. Cal closed his eyes and tried to imagine where Andy and Rich Isnard were. He hadn't heard from them again. They were on the run and would only make contact if absolutely necessary. For the umpteenth time he wondered how he'd find them. Another problem to figure out enroute.

Cal's initial plan called for him and Daniel to fly to Afghanistan and try to find their friends. Unlike past operations, Cal couldn't use his contacts inside any of the government agencies operating in the Middle East. There was no telling who could be trusted, or worse, who was compromised.

That left few options, but that was fine with Cal. He and Daniel were used to working as an independent unit. They'd make do. Marines always did.

A double honk from the far side of the runway flicked him from his thoughts. Two vehicles sped his way. He frowned when he recognized them. He didn't want a sendoff party. The first was MSgt Willy Trent's enormous lava-red Ford truck. 550? 650? Cal couldn't remember. They seemed to be getting bigger and bigger every time the huge Marine bought a new one. This one looked more like a tow truck than a privately owned vehicle. It was something a well-to-do redneck might drive instead of the near seven foot tall black man.

The second vehicle was a midnight blue BMW X5M. It belonged to Jonas, who Cal could now see was behind the wheel. The guy could afford a fleet of vehicles and chauffeurs, but insisted on driving his one and only automobile himself. Cal had to respect the billionaire for that. One of many reasons he liked the guy.

The two vehicles pulled into the parking spaces next to the hangar, both marked PRIVATE. Trent was the first out, hopping down from the chest high cab with ease. Cal waved.

"What are you doing here, Top?"

Trent ignored the question and popped open the truck bed, hauling out a rucksack. As he did, more men piled out of both vehicles.

Gaucho alighted from Trent's truck and surprise guests hopped out of Jonas's 550hp ride: Dr. Alvin Higgins, former CIA interrogator extraordinaire, and world-class shrink, was joined by super hacker Neil Patel.

"Would someone please tell me what the hell is going on?" asked Cal while the others grabbed bags from their rides. Neil toted a set of matching Louis Vitton carry-ons while Dr. Higgins carried a weathered doctor's bag and a well-worn leather suitcase.

Jonas threw a hiker pack over one shoulder and locked his SUV. "We thought you might need some help."

That wasn't what Cal wanted to hear. "Guys, I appreciate you coming out, but this is something I need to do alone. Me and Daniel. That's it."

Dr. Higgins adjusted his pearl-rimmed glasses. "Now, Calvin, how could you possibly keep us from visiting such exotic lands? Wasn't that part of the job description?" asked Dr. Higgins in his academic British-laced inflection.

"No offense, Doc, but this ain't exactly a vacation to Bora Bora. Besides, your old employer would have a conniption if they knew you were a part of this. You did hear how they're treating Andy, right?"

Higgins nodded. "It is one of reasons I feel compelled to join you."

"Come on, boss, Andy's a friend of ours too," said Gaucho.

"Yeah, but..."

Trent placed a massive hand on Cal's shoulder. "Best not to fight it, Cal. We're coming."

Cal looked up at his friend and shook his head. "I should've known you'd weasel your way in somehow."

Trent grinned and patted Cal on the back. "You wanna see what the real surprise is?"

"There's more?"

Trent nodded and pointed at Jonas.

"It should be getting here right about....now," said Jonas, turning at the sound of airplane engines. A private jet rolled into view and made its way toward the hangar.

"You know, I may be a lowly grunt, but I have seen a chartered jet before," said Cal.

Trent chuckled. "Just wait."

The aircraft made its way across the runway and turned so that it stopped perpendicular to where they stood. It didn't look all that remarkable to Cal, who honestly couldn't tell one private jet from another. The plane looked new and could probably hold up to ten passengers. He looked back at Jonas.

"I don't get it."

Jonas smiled and pointed to the tail. Cal read the tail number: *TJG911*. It took him a second to figure it out.

The Jefferson Group?

"Did you buy that thing?" asked Cal, shaking his head.

Jonas grinned. "For your information, that *thing* is a Gulfstream G650ER. It's the newest model on the market. With a max range of seventy-five hundred nautical miles, this beauty has the capacity to take you all over the world in one hop."

"And you're saying it's yours?"

"No, it's ours. Official property of The Jefferson Group as of eleven thirty last night. Neil mentioned that we might want to look into getting a more reliable mode of transport, and I've been keeping my eye out for a new ride. Good timing. Now, about the tail number, the *TJG* you recognized, but the 911 on the tail number has dual meanings."

"Let me guess, we're America's new nine one one force?" asked Cal. The slogan had been used to describe the Marine Corps for decades.

"That's the second reference. The first is to your parents."

Cal's parents had died on 9/11. It wasn't something he

talked about, but it was an event that he thought about daily. It was a nice gesture from the newest addition to the team.

"Thanks," Cal said, not knowing what else to say.

"Does that mean you like it?" asked Jonas.

"Yeah, can we keep it, can we keep it?" asked Trent, mimicking a child's voice, even clapping his hands.

Cal laughed. "Screw it. Why not?"

Jonas swept his arm toward their new toy. "Then let me give you the grand tour while the crew preps for takeoff. I'm telling you, Cal, you're gonna love this baby."

LANGLEY, VIRGINIA

6:25AM, AUGUST 24TH

The office was like something out of a luxury design magazine. *Architectural Digest* would've had a field day had they known the place existed. Every knickknack had its place. A three-inch-thick glass table here, a delicate porcelain vase there. Reclaimed barn wood planks criss-crossed the once bland ceiling that was now painted gravel gray. The faint scent of fresh mint. Not a smudge or a speck of dust. That probably had something to do with the fact that the cleaning staff was required to service the spacious office no less than twice a day, including weekends.

Kingsley Coles liked things his way and no other. He could remember few times in his life when things hadn't turned out the way he planned. He'd paid for every upgrade in his office out of his personal funds, of which he had plenty. It was a matter of pride, not vanity. When visitors entered his sanctum, they got an instant feel for the man lording over it. Precise. Level. Commanding.

So as he sat back in his silver Herman Miller chair, he had little doubt how the current situation would unfold.

Afghanistan was a mess and he had two rogue officers to prove it. While he didn't like Rich Isnard's tactics, the Baghdad station chief had a way of getting things done. Coles respected that. As long as Isnard hadn't strayed too far outside the gray area, the deputy director NCS let his underling play. There were numerous successes tucked under the man's belt.

But this time he'd gone too far. Not only had he disappeared, he'd done so in order to consort with Major B. Andrews, USMC. Coles had never met the Marine, but what he saw in the man's official Marine Corps record spoke of a career officer who was not only professional but respected by his superiors and his subordinates. Having the Navy Cross didn't hurt. Coles suspected that he might have actually enjoyed meeting the Marine if the current situation didn't exist. They were cut from a similar cloth.

None of that mattered now. He was officially no longer under the purview of Kingsley Coles, at least on paper. But now that the two Marines were in cahoots, they were very much Coles's problem. To make matters worse, the idiots had stumbled onto an operation that was years in the making. Something he had taken a personal interest in. Coles would not let it be ruined by two simpletons who just didn't know when to keep their noses out of places they didn't belong.

The deputy director matched the cadence of the ticking clock mounted above the door with his blinking eyes. It was his way of getting back in rhythm, in sync. A soft breath in and hard breath out. Meditation without the spiritual nonsense.

His mind wandered back to the task at hand. The one-time environmental lawyer was not used to having the CIA director, the inspector general AND the president breathing down his neck. It was more than a nuisance. It was a problem that had to go away.

Coles picked up his phone and dialed a number from memory. He let it ring once then hung up. He dialed the number again and the call was answered immediately.

"Yes, sir?"

"Where are we on taking care of the problem?" asked Coles, tracing his pinky along the edge of his two hundred year old oak desk, happy that no dust remained.

"We'll be landing in two hours."

"Have you activated our assets?"

"Yes."

"Good. I think you're going to have a bit of company."

"Who?"

"I don't know yet. Just call it a hunch," said Coles, once again replaying the conversation with President Zimmer and his chief of staff Travis Haden. There'd been something in Haden's eyes that told Coles the SEAL wasn't happy with the CIA's response. He seemed like just the type of person who had contacts that got things done, namely direct action when needed. Another wrinkle that Coles had his people looking into.

"ETA?"

"They could be there now or they may just be leaving the east coast. I don't know. I should know more soon."

The man on the other end, a twenty-one year CIA veteran named Anthony Farrago, grunted. He understood what Coles was saying. Be prepared for anything. Farrago was used to the deputy director's vague orders. It was the way Coles did business, give your men just enough information and let them figure the rest out. The good ones soared while the subpar floundered. It made it easy to weed out the ranks.

Coles knew that Farrago liked it that way. The dour spook was best on his own, or at least with a very long leash. He was the deputy director's utility man, the guy who just got things done. With contacts all over the Middle East, and wounds from more than a dozen battles, Farrago was Coles's weapon of choice. He knew how to keep his mouth shut too.

"I'll call you when we get in," said Farrago.

Coles ended the call and set his phone on the desk. A piece of paper had been moved slightly by the air coming out of the overhead vent. Coles nudged it back in place, his domain perfect once again.

Despite his heavy workload, he knew he had to pay special attention to this operation. With an untold number of missions being conducted around the globe, Coles had his fingers in many pies. Much like a master carpenter, he knew where each of his pieces lay and their direct effect on the whole. Isnard and Andrews were two of the pieces that had to go.

Since accepting the prestigious post, Coles had slashed and burned his way to a more streamlined intelligence gathering apparatus. You might not like his caustic style, but few would dare to discount his effectiveness. Simply put, when Kingsley Coles wanted something done, it was done. He took his responsibilities seriously.

GERESHK, AFGHANISTAN

3:02PM AFT, AUGUST 24TH

They'd somehow made it to Gereshk in one piece. Along the way, Isnard used his seemingly endless supply of cash to buy Andy clothes. That, along with an ample dousing of road dust, transformed the Marine into just another tired and dirty face in the desert landscape.

After the chase and the near miss with the Marine attack helicopters, Isnard's security detachment bolted. The survivors told Isnard not to call them again. The Marines were on their own. That fact didn't seem to bother the spook. Isnard's outward calm helped settle Andy's nerves. The days of captivity were finally catching up to him. He felt weak and it was an effort to put one foot in front of another. Isnard didn't push, letting Andy take a breather when needed.

Andy wasn't one to complain, but he felt the limits of his physical strength waning. Even though there was plenty of food to be had in the makeshift shacks along the way, he couldn't find the appetite to eat. He forced himself to drink, remembering the nights in his OCS squad bay, chugging canteens full of water as his sergeant instructors watched. The order always included hoisting your overturned canteen over your head to prove that you'd finished it all. That was one way to keep your charges hydrated.

His stomach grumbled from whatever parasite had laid claim to his insides. Hopefully his bowels could stay intact until they reached Kandahar. Isnard led the way into another tent. They'd struck out in the last five. What they needed was transportation, having ditched their delivery van on the outskirts of Gereshk.

Kandahar was barely a two hour drive away along Highway 1, but the damn road was wide open. They couldn't risk going alone. They needed to be part of a larger convoy. Lots of people. Lots of goods moving from point A to point B.

Andy was proud of his half-stuttering Pashtun, but he marveled at Isnard's command of the language. The guy knew the people and the language. Within minutes the young man sitting behind a short wooden table invited the two Marines to an early dinner.

"You're going to Kandahar?" Isnard asked his new friend.

"Yes."

"How many vehicles?"

"Twenty five, my friend. Would you like a ride?" the man asked, his eyebrow lifted as if asking to be in on Isnard's secret.

Isnard nodded. "If it wouldn't be too much trouble. We lost our car a mile back. Axle."

The man nodded with a knowing smile. Driving in Afghanistan wasn't like driving down Main Street U.S.A. There were potholes everywhere. Sometimes whole portions of road just disappeared. It was part of the Afghan way of life, move around and keep going. The people had learned to adapt.

"Just the two?"

"Yes."

"Do you want to know how much?"

Isnard shrugged as if it didn't matter. "You are a friend. As a friend I know you'll give us a fair price."

The man smiled, his gold canine peeking out from his sagging mustache. "You know how to shoot a rifle?"

Again the shrug from Isnard. "Who doesn't?"

The man nodded, scratching his scraggly beard, thinking.

"I give you a deal. Ride in the lead vehicle and help protect my goods from bandits and crooked police, and I give you half price."

Andy didn't like it. He wasn't sure what the full price would be, but he was sure Isnard was good for it. The better play was to hunker down in one of the twenty five vehicles and stay out of sight. It wasn't that Andy was scared of being shot at or shooting someone else, but being seen wasn't something they needed right now.

After a moment to think, Isnard said, "We'd be happy to help, my friend."

The two men shook hands.

"Please, call me Latif. Latif Saladin."

THEY WAITED UNTIL DARK TO LEAVE, THEIR HOST explaining that checkpoint guards tended to be lazier after nightfall. He was right. An hour in they'd made it through three checkpoints without more than a cursory glance at whatever lay inside the packed cargo holds. Andy was pretty sure it had more to do with the money he saw Latif slipping the guards along with other sundry items from the salesman's eclectic collection. He wondered how many pockets the man had under his billowy robe.

As they cruised along, Andy's mind wandered back to the

last time he'd been in-country. Then he'd been part of a beefed up convoy of Marine light armored vehicles (LAVs) who'd offered to give him and his squad leader a lift to Kandahar. There'd been no one to stop them. Hell, they'd even had gunships and drones providing overwatch as they moved. No such protection this time. Now it was Andy, Isnard, Latif, and his complement of some forty employees. Most looked to be no more than fifteen, but every one came armed and grim faced.

The number of weapons did little to settle Andy's nerves. They were still in the middle of Afghanistan being pursued by a force that could easily overwhelm the ragtag convoy.

"This remind you of playing cowboys and indians as a kid?" Isnard asked over the heavy revving of their vehicle's engine.

"Feels more like General Custer's last stand. Circle the wagons, right?"

Isnard laughed. "Hey, man, if I'm going out, I'm going out shooting. But I'm not a proud bastard like Custer. I know when to duck and run."

That much Andy knew. While Isnard did, on the surface, look like a reckless operator, the guy was much more than most people probably realized. He was a survivor, a winner. It was what made him such a good spook. He was always analyzing the situation behind those bored eyes, tearing plans apart and rebuilding on the fly. Much like Cal Stokes, Rich Isnard inspired confidence in his men. It was probably the only reason Andy had made the decision to leave his post at 8th & I. Well, that and a bit of adventure. The life of a newly minted Marine major was more paper-pusher than behind-the-lines operator. It was why so many of his peers left the Corps after their first tour as captains. Going from company commander to desk jockey didn't sit well with hard-charging grunts.

Isnard nudged Andy and pointed to the road ahead.

"Another checkpoint."

"This one looks bigger," said Andy, noticing the presence of high powered lights blazing in the night. Different than the last three posts that had had not much more than a rusty streetlight and a couple guys with flashlights.

The convoy slowed as it approached, the screech of brakes bringing them to a stuttering stop.

Andy's heart beat a little faster as he squinted through the spotlights and saw what lay within the checkpoint perimeter. Instead of a collection of dented Afghan police and military vehicles, he saw the familiar outlines of humvees and armored SUVs.

Andy watched as Latif walked out in front of his caravan and approached the cluster of guards. They seemed casual enough, all smoking cigarettes, weapons slung over their shoulders. Latif kept his distance, talking and gesturing with his hands like the good salesman he was. This time no money or goods were exchanged.

A minute later, Latif walked up to the passenger side door of their truck.

"They want us all out of the trucks. Inspection." His face seemed placid, but something in his eyes rang alarm bells in Andy's head. "Come. Help me tell the others."

Isnard and Andy climbed down and followed the Afghan as he went from truck to truck instructing his men to turn off their engines and step to the side of the road. Once they'd made it to the final vehicle, Latif went around the back of the last canvas-flapped truck bed. The Marines followed.

"They are looking for two Americans. They say the men are criminals, possibly terrorists trying to destroy our country. There is even a reward for their capture."

No accusation in his tone or in his gaze. More like a flash

of amusement. Andy could tell that this man lived for adventure.

"We are Americans," said Isnard.

"Are you the men they are looking for?"

"What if we are?"

Latif gave a slight shrug, leaning against the back of the truck. "It could be that we have more in common than I thought."

"Oh?"

"I know those vehicles, my friend. Not police, not military. They are government, possibly secret police." Latif spit on the ground.

"We could leave," offered Isnard, pointing to the darkness beyond the road.

Latif shook his head. "I like you, my friend. Something tells me that I would gain more by helping you than turning you in. The government pays little for criminals, the secret police even less. Tell me, would you return the favor?"

"On my honor as a United States Marine," said Isnard, putting his hand out.

Latif's eyebrows rose, but he took Isnard's hand in his, even covering the clasp with a second hand.

"You are a long way from home, Marine. Come, let us see how we can get out of this mess."

Nods from each man. Just as they went to join the others, there was shouting from the front of the convoy. Andy saw that one of Latif's young guards was pinned against a truck, his weapon lying on the ground. Andy knew what had happened before snippets of the yelling made it to his ears.

The interrogators, four men in suits, turned as the hoisted teenager pointed to the back of the convoy. Every one of them turned, their eyes locking on to Latif, Isnard and Andy.

Isnard grabbed Andy's arm. "Time to go."

ENROUTE TO KANDAHAR, AFGHANISTAN

8:02PM AFT, AUGUST 24TH

Another surprise waited Cal and the rest of The Jefferson Group after lifting off from Charlottesville. The first came in the form of recently retired Chief Warrant Officer Benny Fletcher, USA. Fletcher had the boyish features of a college cheerleader, not a retired CWO-3. He greeted them all formally like a general's steward.

"I met Benny passing through Fort Campbell last month," explained Jonas Layton. "I got turned around and he offered to show me the way back to my conference. I returned the favor with lunch and one thing led to another."

"Fort Campbell? What did he do before retiring?" asked Cal. He was familiar with Ft. Campbell, having spent much of his adulthood in Nashville. Ft. Campbell is approximately an hour from downtown Nashville.

"He was a Night Stalker."

The "Night Stalkers" are formally known as the 160th Special Operations Aviation Regiment (Airborne). They first cut their teeth in Grenada in the 1980s and soon built a reputation for their night flying abilities, hence their name. They'd been used extensively since 9/11 in special operations roles.

"Really? And you hired him as a flight attendant?"

"Not exactly. I learned a long time ago that when you run into talent, like top notch talent, you hire them first and figure out the rest later. Benny said he'd be happy to help until we found him something better suited for his skill set."

It was the same way Cal's father ran SSI. Find the good ones and never let them go.

"Besides, it never hurts to have a third pilot," said Jonas.

"Where'd you find the other two?"

Jonas turned his head toward the galley. "Hey, Benny, you mind taking over up front? Send the brothers back?"

"No problem, Mr. Layton."

"You're gonna have to cut the mister crap if you want to stick around this motley crew."

Benny smiled, even blushing. "Okay...Jonas."

Cal leaned over and asked, "Brothers?"

Jonas put up a finger indicating that the answer was forthcoming. A minute later two men walked out of the cockpit. Cal watched them, curious. You could tell they were brothers, same chestnut hair, all-American good looks, probably six foot. Not twins but familial features for sure. They could've been military aviation poster models in their *TJG* monogrammed polo shirts.

"Cal, I'd like you to meet Jim and Johnny Powers. Gentlemen, for all intents and purposes, this is your boss, Cal Stokes."

Cal stood and shook their hands. Firm grips. Military, a cautious look from Jim and a mischievous grin from Johnny. Cal noticed a thin scar running the length of Johnny's jawline. War wound or childhood prank?

"Jim, Johnny and Jonas?" Cal asked, giving Jonas an amused look.

Jonas raised his palms with a shrug.

"Why Jim and not Jimmy?" asked Cal, trying to gauge their personalities.

Johnny Powers answered for his brother. "He used to go by Jimmy until he went into the Corps. Thought Jim sounded more dignified." He mimed sipping a cup of tea with his pinky finger out.

Jim gave his brother a dirty look, but grinned. "It's true. I blurted my nickname the first day of OCS and got reamed. After that I always introduced myself as Jim." He shrugged like it was neither a good or bad thing, just something he'd done and rolled with ever since. "Jonas tells us you're Marine."

Cal nodded. "Seems like a long time ago. When did you get out?"

"A year ago. Finished my commitment and bumped into Jonas on a private hop to Dubai. The rest, as they say, is history."

"What did you fly in the Corps?" asked Cal, warming to the brothers.

"Started on Hueys then moved over to Ospreys. Spent most of my time at Cherry Point flying over Lejeune."

"And what about you? Another Marine?" Cal asked Johnny.

Johnny shook his head vehemently. "No way. Big brother was the one with the stick up his ass. Nope, Air Force all the way. I flew AC-130 Spookies, you know, the gunships."

"What he's not telling you is that he was a member of the Air Force Special Operations Command (AFSOC), specifically the First Special Operations Wing out of Hurlburt Field. These guys have spent more time over the desert than Lawrence of Arabia did in it."

Cal was impressed. Two, no three (he'd have to chat with Benny later) high speed aviators. Most people thought that fighter pilots were the tough guys, the real flying heroes. But Cal knew differently, and apparently so did Jonas. It took big balls to fly a squad of Marines into a hot landing zone. The same thing with the AFSOC pilots. Tasked with supporting special operations troops, they were the elite of the elite despite flying the comparatively unsexy AC-130 gunships. Cal had seen the big bird in action and was more than impressed.

Suddenly it all came together, what Jonas had set in motion. They didn't call him The Fortuneteller for nothing. Without a word from Cal, the brilliant billionaire had added to their army. By hiring the three aviators, Jonas effectively gave The Jefferson Group all the air support they'd need. Need someone to fly a helo, gotcha covered. Commercial airliner? No problem. Hell, aside from fighter jets, which Cal figured they'd never get their hands on anyway, they now had the talent to fly anything. He had to hand it to Jonas. One of the best indications of a man's worth is what he does when you're not watching. The guy was good, really good.

"How much do you know about what we're doing?" Cal asked the brothers.

Jim looked to Jonas who nodded. "Jonas said we're going in to pick up a couple of Jarheads, under the radar."

Part of Cal was annoyed that Jonas had said that much, but then he realized that if these guys were going to work for him they might as well know, but they had to get the speech now.

"True. What I'm about to tell you is so over the level of Top Secret there is no classification. The Jefferson Group is a presidentially sanctioned organization tasked with..."

CAL GAVE THEM THE FIVE THOUSAND FOOT VIEW. WHAT

the president wanted them to do, some of what they'd accomplished over the previous months, and finally why they were on their way to Afghanistan. He included what would happen to them should they divulge The Jefferson Group's true mission, namely a lifetime incarcerated in solitary confinement. That or a bullet to the head.

There was silence for a moment as the Powers brothers digested the information. Then, to Cal's surprise, they turned to each other, Johnny smiling wide, Jim more casual. Simultaneously they raised a hand and smacked a high five, just like they were on a baseball field and one of them had done a diving catch at short.

"I told you!" said Johnny.

Jim shrugged.

Cal looked at Jonas, suppressing a smile. "Well, I guess they're in. Now, if we only knew what Andy and Rich were up to."

SOMEWHERE ALONG HIGHWAY 1

BETWEEN GERESHK AND KANDAHAR, AFGHANISTAN - 8:05PM AFT, AUGUST 24TH

First came the shouting, enemies ordering their subordinates to rush the convoy. Then came the swivel of spotlights, illuminating the dusty night air, seeking out the Americans. Finally came the unmistakable revving of humvee engines, the assault was coming.

Latif pulled the two Americans around the left side of the truck, away from the enemy. "We must get to the fifth vehicle."

There was a lot of space between them and the fifth vehicle, lots of time to be found and killed.

"Why?" asked Isnard, crouching low to look under the product laden truck.

"You will see."

Isnard looked up at the Afghan. "Fine. I'll go first."

It was decided that Andy would bring up the rear. While he usually might have protested, he wasn't too proud to admit that in his weakened state he really shouldn't be walking point.

More shouting, large tires crunching their way closer. Heavy machine guns undoubtedly ready, waiting for the Americans to poke their heads out.

Three vehicles up, Isnard stopped, cocking his head to the side, listening. His head snapped around, a furtive glance to his companions, then he was flat on his stomach, crawling under the truck. Andy and Latif followed.

Crowded behind the front right tire, the three men watched as Latif's men were ordered to their knees, hands on their heads. Only one man, a boy really, resisted, receiving a crushing blow to the head from his aggressor's rifle. The boy crumpled. Andy knew he was dead.

If there was any hesitation in Andy to fire on Afghan forces, it left him a moment later. The same military and police units he and thousands of coalition troops had trained, men who'd sworn to uphold liberty and freedom, leveled their weapons. Every one of Latif's men were cut down by not one but two humvee mounted machine guns along with the ground troops. In twenty seconds it was over. Andy knew because he felt and counted each one. *Tick, tick, tick...*

Latif pounded the ground with his fist, letting out a barely audible moan. Pure anguish. A common smuggler with transient contractors didn't mourn. Andy knew in that extended moment that Latif had family in the pile of murdered boys. Family now gone forever.

Something in the Marine snapped. Any weariness he'd felt left him. It was like the air throbbed, thumping in his ears.

His gaze met Isnard's. They nodded and shuffled back the way they'd come.

With Latif regaining his composure and now bringing up the rear, the three men snuck from shadow to shadow. It was only a matter of time before the opposition came around to their side of the convoy, but for now they were being cautious. The bastards called to them, threatening and taunting. As if they'd just throw up their hands in surrender after seeing so many killed so quickly. They didn't know the Marines they were dealing with.

The familiar adrenaline rush coursed through Andy's veins, smell, vision and touch all heightened, drop by drop the bucket filled. Somehow they made it to the fifth vehicle, Latif scrambling in the cargo flap. It felt like forever before the merchant's head popped out, followed by his hands holding a pair of rocket propelled grenades (RPGs). The Marines each took one, prepping the weapons without thinking.

In under a minute the three men had twelve RPGs stacked on the ground and three more in their hands. The tricky part was going to be the back blast. More than a few idiots had killed comrades by thinking nothing was coming out the back.

"We need to get on top of the trucks," said Andy, realizing that the tightly parked trucks offered no other room. Isnard nodded and was the first up, keeping his profile low.

Louder shouting and more vehicles. Their time was running out. When Andy finally got his footing on top of the canvas cargo top, he was sure the ancient fabric was about to give way. It was like walking on thin ice, peril a footstep away.

He ignored caution and was the first to stand, the only way he could get a clear shot and compensate for the weapon's back blast. *Whooosh!* He dropped to his belly reaching for another RPG.

Men scattered at the telltale sound, the explosion rocking the check point. *Whooosh! Whooosh!* Rich then Latif launched their RPGs, the heavy rounds slamming into humvees. Take out the big guns first.

It was pure chaos on the ground, but the enemy knew where they were. With time limited, Andy was the only one who had time to launch one more, before the three men slipped off the backside of the vehicle, bullets following, chests heaving.

"Now what?" asked Andy.

They'd taken out a couple vehicles and a few men, but there were plenty more who were converging on their hiding spot.

A look passed between the three men. Defiant but resigned to their fate. Surrender wasn't an option.

"Let's go," said Isnard, turning and heading toward the sound of crackling fire, and angry shouts.

He took out two men with his first burst, Andy another with his. They fanned out, walking right down the side of the road like heroes in an old western. Wyatt Earp and his boys taking on the cowboys at the O.K. Corral.

Latif was the first to be hit, a stinger in his right arm. He grunted and kept moving, shifting his weapon to his left hand, disciplined fire.

There were targets everywhere and even more rounds flying overhead. A tiny part of Andy's subconscious couldn't believe he hadn't been shot yet. It was only a matter of time. But the rounds kept coming, flying high, bad aim.

Then he saw them. A line of black SUVs, heads peeking out from behind. None of those guys were shooting. As soon as Andy wondered why the answer came. They were letting the lowly Afghan police take the casualties and hoping they would kill the Americans. Cowards. The thought made Andy smile despite the intense heat of the burning vehicles he was trying get cover behind.

More small arms fire. Luckily they'd taken out the humvees. Andy hated to think what it would feel like with MK19 rounds in the mix.

Isnard sprinted to the next bit of cover, a blasted humvee door, when Andy's blood went cold. *BOOM! BOOM!*

All three men dropped to the deck, waiting for the explosions to take them out. But that didn't happen. Instead the black SUVs disappeared, reappearing moments later several feet away, fiery hulks. *BOOM! BOOM!*

The front of Latif's convoy exploded a split second later.

Those are tank rounds, thought Andy. Whatever it was, the few remaining Afghans bolted for any vehicle that wasn't burning and took off down the highway.

Without the sound of gunfire, the area fell still. There was the snapping and popping of smoldering vehicles, and the death moan of some unseen combatant, but they'd come out relatively unscathed.

As Isnard wrapped a piece of his torn T-shirt around Latif's upper arm, Andy waited. Soon came the rattle and crunch of tracked vehicles. It wasn't the hum of an Abrams, he knew that for sure. It was the squeaky turn of ancient parts, the rough screech of gears changing. Not Americans.

He had to find a vehicle and get them away from the check point. Walking wasn't an option. Any half-ass newbie could track them down, even at night, what with the limited cover in the low lying desert. But every vehicle Andy came to was either burning or disabled, courtesy of the gun battle.

The engine noises rumbled closer as he climbed down from yet another dead truck. Nothing to do but wait. Like most Marines, Andy hated waiting. He didn't have to wait long. Rolling into the light of the remaining spotlights came four rust-lined Russian tanks. They sagged under their age, like old men taking one last walk into the sunset.

They lined up in a row just off the highway, idling. Then came the sound of footfalls, steps coming from behind. Andy's eyes went wide. Streaming onto the road were tens, then hundreds of armed men, all dressed like desert vagabonds, nomads, faces hidden, robes scraping the pavement as they surrounded the caravan.

Two men broke off from the others and headed to where Andy now stood with Isnard and Latif. They carried AK-47s pointed at the ground. They stopped a few feet away, first one then the other pulling down the fabric covering their faces. Both men had deep set eyes. Men of the desert. Deeply tanned crow's feet. Their facial hair blotted out every other aspect of their features. Andy immediately pegged them as Kochi, traditionally nomadic people. The problem was that many of the Kochi people, whether out of ignorance or necessity, had aligned themselves with the Taliban.

"Which one of you is Isnard?" one of the men asked in Pashtun.

Isnard stepped forward.

"And that is Andrews?"

"It is," replied Isnard.

"And that man?" the larger of the two men asked, pointing at Latif.

"A friend," said Isnard. "And you?"

"We are guardians of the desert," the man replied grandly, spreading his arms wide.

"May I call you friend?" asked Isnard.

The two strangers exchanged glances. Number two stranger nodded. "You may call us friends, Isnard. Come. We must leave before the army arrives."

With their only option standing in front of them, supported by what Andy estimated to be two hundred men and old yet precise tanks, the three men accepted the escort. No one told them to relinquish their weapons and they were offered water from ragged goat bladders. Once satiated, the troop moved off into the night. Andy wondered if it was just another death march. Out of one boiling cauldron and into another.

KANDAHAR, AFGHANISTAN

12:11AM AFT, AUGUST 25TH

Anthony Farrago swore under his breath. Not only had that prick Rich Isnard slipped through the incompetent fingers of the Afghan police, military AND their intelligence force, they'd done it four hours before . The moron on the other end of the conversation kept going on and on about a rebel division swooping down in the middle of the night. He wasn't making any sense.

Farrago knew from long experience that Arabs had the bad habit of overstating enemy forces. That was especially the case if said forces overwhelmed their own. *Cowards and liars*.

He'd heard enough. "You listen to me. Tell your boss that not another penny will go into his account if he doesn't find those two."

More blathering on the other end. Excuses. Promises. Empty words.

"Just do it," Farrago growled.

Anthony Farrago hadn't risen to the right hand of a deputy director of the CIA by being nice. Sure his attitude had bit him in the ass more than once, but that's what fiery Italian-Americans did, bawl people out every once in a while. If that meant stomping on a few toes and chewing some ass, Farrago was only too happy to comply.

Even though he felt like he was on the wrong side of fifty when he looked in the mirror every morning, the career spook knew he had plenty of years left. Three marriages and four stints in rehab later, Farrago had come up the hard way. From the frozen streets of Minneapolis to a tour in the Navy, and finally to where he hoped to die: The Central Intelligence Agency.

He'd begun his CIA career as an embassy staffer in Rome, learning the ropes from a crusty station chief who'd cut his teeth on the front lines of Moscow during the Cold War. They'd become friends and for a while Farrago was the golden child, gathering contacts and spies like the Pied Piper.

He was in high demand and spent time all over the world until finally settling in the Middle East. After 9/11 there'd been so much work that he rarely saw home, hence the repeated attempts at marriage and occasional relapse into the bottle. Each time the CIA picked him up, dusted him off, then sent him on to the next thing.

Now he lived on the road, relishing the freedom, spurning long-term relationships in exchange for life-or-death intrigue. Along the way he'd slipped a couple times. His mouth did have a way of interjecting at the wrong time. He'd written them off as minor mistakes, but in truth they'd derailed his aspirations of becoming a station chief. That's what he'd always wanted. Lord of the manor. Now Farrago was damaged goods, but not damaged enough to get the boot. He'd gotten the ultimatum from Kingsley Coles himself, "Work for me or you're out."

The position started out as more of an administrative role, something Farrago hated. But he soon came to see the political appointee just wanted to get a better feel for the headstrong Italian. Within months, Farrago was on the road every other week, then three weeks out of each month. Courier deliveries led to inspections which morphed into what he was doing now, anything he wanted.

He was given autonomy and the resources to do what had to be done. Coles didn't want to know all the details and that was fine with Farrago. Left alone he was a cunning operator, flexing his muscles as needed. He liked the variety and the power. Who wouldn't?

Like this operation. It was exactly what Farrago wanted. A guy like Rich Isnard was too young and inexperienced to be a station chief. Sure the kid was good, but Baghdad? No way. Things had to be corrected and Farrago would spearhead the effort. The Agency had gotten soft. It was time to put a boot in certain orifices.

Isnard and that Marine, Andrews, had gone too far, encroached on his turf. Sure he'd twisted a few truths and doctored a couple of reports, but that was all part of the game, part of his job. Coles understood. There was a bigger picture to take into account. Upstarts like Isnard and Andrews didn't get that. They were Boy Scouts in a den of howling wolves. Farrago was the alpha male tasked with fixing the problem.

There were multiple fronts to fight. It was all part of the fun. He'd give the Afghans one more day to find Isnard and Andrews. Farrago would personally oversee the rest.

He looked at his watch. Probably another thirty minutes. Farrago leaned back against his dented loaner, his tongue running along his upper lip in anticipation. A beer or shot of rum would be nice, but he'd sworn off the stuff. Too bad.

He exhaled.

The runway was quiet for now. In thirty minutes it would be Ground Zero.

* * *

12:34AM

The Gulfstream touched down, its occupants feeling barely a thump as every tire settled.

"Welcome to Kandahar, ladies and gents. Thanks for flying *TJG* airlines. Don't forget to tip your waiter."

Everyone chuckled at Johnny Power's announcement. It was the last of many they'd heard over the preceding hours. The guy was a bottomless well of wit.

There'd been plenty of time on the flight over to get acquainted with the new team members. The three pilots rotated every other hour, coming to the back when they weren't flying. The three men, even the quiet Benny Fletcher, were going to fit in nicely. Cal understood the simple fact that, because they were once again part of a pseudo-military unit, it made the men happy. He was pretty sure they'd accept a lot less pay just to be onboard.

Not that Cal would think of paying them less. If the last three years were any indication, what Cal and his team did was dangerous. He was happy to have the ability to pay his men handsomely. They deserved it.

"Cal, can you come up to the cockpit?" came Jim's voice over the speaker system.

Cal unlatched his seat belt and made his way to the front. Jim turned when the reinforced cockpit door opened.

"You expecting company?" he asked, pointing into the hazy night.

Cal bent at the waist and looked out the thick glass

window. The runway was still except for a vehicle flashing its headlights in the middle of the tarmac.

"Did you talk to the tower?" asked Cal.

"Yeah. They don't know anything about the truck."

The plane slowed as it neared the vehicle. There were two men standing outside their respective doors. Cal squinted.

"I'll be damned."

"You recognize them?" asked Johnny Powers.

"Yeah. Can you open one of these windows?"

"Uh huh. Here, switch with me."

Jim opened the side window and swapped places with Cal. Cal stuck his head out the window.

"To what do we have the honor of Her Majesty's finest?" he shouted over the engine noise.

Gene Kreyling was an easily recognizable figure. Gray eyepatch over one eye, the gruff British operator stood like an iron golem. He'd been part of Cal's operation to stamp out ISIS earlier that month. Their relationship had started contentiously, but Cal now considered the brusque warrior part of the family. The man on the other side of the truck was Kreyling's number two, Rango.

Kreyling didn't say anything, just motioned for the plane to follow them. Cal nodded and popped back in the window.

"What's that about?" asked Johnny.

Cal didn't have a clue. No one was supposed to know they were coming. The last he'd heard Kreyling had been tasked with helping the U.N. train its new anti-terrorism reaction force. Hell, he'd recommended him for it. President Zimmer, the architect of the Zimmer Doctrine and the newly formed reaction force, was more than happy to forward Cal's recommendation to the general commanding the team.

Not that he wasn't happy to see his friends, but the fact that they'd been waiting was more than a little unsettling. Who else knew they were coming?

"Follow that truck," Cal told the pilots. "Oh, and make sure you're ready to take off if we need to."

The Powers brother exchanged questioning looks as if to say, "Is this what it's always like with these guys?"

KANDAHAR, AFGHANISTAN

As the minutes slipped by, Anthony Farrago's frustration clicked higher. There'd only been one landing in the last hour and that was on an auxiliary strip on the farthest edge of the tarmac. He couldn't make out the markings thanks to the haze and gloom. The runway lighting was just barely acceptable for night use. Seeing anything from afar was impossible.

The control tower manager had assured Farrago that the American plane was going to land and taxi to this exact spot. No phone calls to say differently. Farrago resisted the urge to call the tower. Instead he walked around his sedan and found his men waiting behind a shoulder high concrete wall. Eighteen men. Private contractors. Experienced men. All of Afghan descent.

He'd used them before. They weren't as good as American contractors, but they knew the land and did jobs for a tenth of what American contractors would. These guys knew their place, mostly because they had nowhere else to go.

Kicked out of various Afghan agencies for a wide range of offenses ranging from drunkenness to rape, they were the scum their country no longer wanted. Perfect for what Farrago had in mind.

"I'm going up to the tower. Keep on eye out for the airplane," Farrago told the team leader, a hulking man with one ear and a jagged scar across his forehead.

The man nodded and went back to puffing on his cigarette. Farrago left the mercenaries, criminals really. He knew a guy like Kingsley Coles would never associate with such men, but they were right up Farrago's alley. Ruthless. Uncaring. Expendable.

Despite his impatience, he smiled as he made his way up to the tower to see what was taking so long. It was only a matter of time before he let his hounds loose.

* * *

KREYLING LED THE GULFSTREAM OFF THE AUXILIARY runway and into a portion of the airport that looked abandoned. The hangar was large enough to accommodate something twice their size, but its doors looked like they were about to fall off and the roof probably did little to keep the weather out.

The Brit met Cal at the bottom of the steps.

"I wasn't expecting to see you," Cal said. "What's going on?"

"Me and Rango were in town as advanced party for the U.N. Ran into some old S.A.S. pals who caught wind of some CIA operation going down tonight."

CIA?

"What's that got to do with us?"

"I ignored it at first but then some drunk Afghan spouted

off about *Jefferson* something. That got my attention. You don't hear the natives mentioning that kind of name. So I bought him a drink, and he starts bragging about some rich bastard his team is going to take down. He finally remembered the name of the rich guy's company, The Jefferson Group."

Cal froze. Kreyling was one of maybe thirty people, including twenty of Cal's own men and the president, who knew The Jefferson Group's real mission.

"And then what happened?"

"I left and started asking around. A few pounds got me what I needed. They were planning on taking you right after landing."

"And you're saying it's a CIA operation?"

Kreyling nodded.

"You hear who's in charge?"

"Some American, but no one knew his name. He's been in country before. Apparently knows people inside the Afghan government."

They'd been on the ground for less than five minutes and were already in the thick of it.

"Can you get us out of here?" asked Cal.

"Your people? Sure. The plane, no."

"What do we do with the plane?"

"How good is your pilot?"

"Very."

"Then he might just have a chance of leaving, but he has to go right now."

There went their way out. Cal was sure that the Powers brothers could find a safe place to wait, possibly the UAE or Bahrain.

"Fine. Give me a minute to brief my guys and then we'll go."

Kreyling nodded and left the drab hangar. Cal joined his

men and told them about the situation. Although more than one team member's eyebrows rose, no one interrupted.

"Doc, I think you and Neil should go with the plane. Things might get hairy."

Dr. Higgins lips pursed. "Calvin, I assure you that I am more than capable of fending for myself." Illustrating the point, Higgins pulled a pistol out of some unseen holster in his back waistband. Cal had never seen the genial psychologist armed, but by the way the good doctor was handling the weapon, it looked like he was no novice. He should've known that Higgins's former employer, the Central Intelligence Agency, would train their lead interrogator in basic combat skills.

That thought gave Cal an idea.

"Hey, doc, you familiar with any current spooks with extensive experience in Afghanistan?"

"It has been a few years, but yes, I probably know the more important players."

"Do you think you could help us narrow down the list if we got a physical description?"

Cal knew it was a long shot, but without Isnard and Andy in hand, they were going to need all the help they could get.

"I will do my best."

"Great. You're in. Now, the rest of us need to go. Take care of my new baby," Cal said to the pilots who were standing at the top of the steps.

"You've got our number. Call us when you need us."

Cal nodded to his newest team members and picked up his pack. Would there ever be an operation when the plan didn't crumble as soon as they'd stepped off? If his time in the Marine Corps taught him anything it was that a plan rarely kept its original form as soon as you said "Go." *Par for the course.*

* * *

Farrago's fist clenched, knuckles cracking. The tower manager backed away slowly, his hand reaching for the black phone mounted to the wall.

"You grab that phone and I break your hand," Farrago said.

The balding airport employee dropped his hands to his sides. Sweat ran down his face, dripping to the ground.

Farrago stepped forward and grabbed the front of the man's stained shirt.

"Now, tell me exactly what happened."

6 MILES SOUTH OF PANJWAI, AFGHANISTAN

12:52AM AFT, AUGUST 25TH

Rich Isnard sat drying his bare feet along the top bank of what was left of the Dori River. The winter melts would replenish the life giving water supply, but now it wasn't more than a trickle. He couldn't see it, but just across the river bed lay the Registan Desert with its red sand hills and rolling desert plains. Isnard swore he could smell the arid expanse, or maybe that was the miles of road dust he now carried on his clothing. Every time he moved a cloud of dust billowed off his body.

Andy was lying next to him, turning fitfully in his sleep. The poor guy's insides were shot. Who knew what bug he'd picked up since being captured? Ever since leaving the check-point hours before, Andy had spent most of the ride hopping off the battered tank to dry heave or drop his pants. He kept a brave face, but Isnard knew Andy was dehydrated and in need of medical attention. By the end of the march, the Marine had stumbled to the ground and passed out. One of the nomads had carried him to where he now lay.

They weren't far from Kandahar, no more than twenty miles as the crow flies. It felt like much more.

While the nomadic tribe treated them with every courtesy, they were also tight-lipped about their destination. Isnard didn't press. Latif was even now talking with the elders, hoping to negotiate a quick trip. At least they were going in the right general direction.

Alone he probably could've made a break for it, somehow made his way to Kandahar. But with Andy in his current condition, there wasn't a chance in hell they'd make it together. He wouldn't leave his fellow Marine behind. No way.

The tribe was spread out over the landscape, the women and children already having prepared bedding and meals. Leaders retired to consult in a sagging tent, the smell of pipe smoke wafting from the open flap. They would call the Marines in soon, or so they'd told him.

He listened to the sweet singing of a group of children nearby, some native nursery rhyme he couldn't place. The lullaby soothed his nerves, trying to erase the last day's journey. Isnard inhaled, savoring the feel, allowing himself a moment to rest.

His reverie ended with the distant drone of aircraft. Helicopters.

They swooped in from the clouds, Russian-made if he had to guess. Maybe friends of his hosts?

The answer came a blink later as shouts filled the night, people running, scattering. Isnard crammed his feet back into his socks and boots. Grabbing his weapon, he went to shake Andy awake, but he was already struggling to his feet. In the dim light his face looked even more sunken.

Both men whipped their gaze toward the still invisible aircraft, making their way along the riverbank. Without warning, three Mi-24 Hinds swooped out of the sky and fired into the center of the encampment. The tanks were the first to go, all four taken out in the first barrage. Turrets flying, the squeal of tearing metal.

Screams from the dying, wails from the running. Those brave enough to stand their ground and return fire were cut down as the two Marines put more distance between them and the slaughter. Given better weapons or even a platoon of men, Isnard would've considered staying. But the attack helicopters, also known as "Flying Tanks" for their heavy armament, were impervious to the pitiful weapons in the hands of the desert tribe.

A plume of raging red reached up to the sky, illuminating the area with a boom. Probably the tribe's fuel trucks.

It was slow going as Isnard kept one arm around Andy, helping him forward. They stumbled and fell. Up again. Crouching in the night, slinking away.

The noise faded. The tribe fled west while the Marine struggled east, toward Kandahar. All alone. Tripping along, the riverbank to their right, daring them to fall once more.

He sensed it before he heard it. The creeping feeling crawling up his back. Aircraft engines powering forward, following, tracking them. Isnard felt the air being sucked out the world. He didn't hesitate, shoving Andy violently toward the river, tumbling end over end to safety, hopefully.

The Marine turned slowly, aimed his inadequate weapon at the sound of the approaching helicopter, and waited.

6 MILES SOUTH OF PANJWAI, AFGHANISTAN

1:03AM AFT, AUGUST 25TH

The Hind came in slowly, a deliberate stalk. She had the ability to blaze across the night sky but she didn't. Its crew knew it had the advantage. A man standing in the open with a submachine gun was no match for the armor and weaponry of the flying arsenal.

The aircraft flared, giving Isnard a momentary glimpse of its underbelly. For some reason he held his shot, still waiting, calculating his next move. He'd faced down warlords, murderers and his fair share of gun barrels in his career, but he'd never stood toe-to-toe with anything like this. A simple trigger pull from their gunners would wipe him off the planet, while his own would probably ding harmlessly off the helo's hull.

Sand swept into his face as the enemy settled onto the ground. Through the grit and wash he could see that every weapon the Hind had was aimed at him. Isnard stood resolute, still sighting down the length of his weapon.

The side hatch opened and a slim figure emerged wearing

a black flight suit and a sophisticated pilot's helmet. Only the man's clean shaven mouth and chin were exposed. Whoever it was wasn't armed and trotted over to where Isnard waited. He was so tempted to blow the guy away after what he'd seen them do to the tribe. But he held his anger, squared his jaw.

"Where is your friend?" the pilot shouted over the helicopter's whine.

"Who are you?"

"There is no time. The others will be back soon. We must get you on board before they return."

It felt like a trap. As soon as they stepped aboard the helo someone was either going to put a bullet in both of their heads or snap cuffs on their wrists. But something in the urgency of the man's tone made Isnard pause. He couldn't see the man's eyes through the helmets tinted visor so he had to rely on body language. Years of dealing with crooks and thieves meant that Rich Isnard was like a one-man lie detector, sensing a person's intent without a word. He'd once estimated that his success rate hovered somewhere around 97%. The other three percent were clinically psychotic.

Life was a gamble. Why not roll the dice one last time?

"He's in the river bed," said Isnard, motioning with his head.

"Come, I will help you get him."

Two minutes later they dragged a dazed and listless Andy up the steep river bank and into the helicopter. Mud caked the side of his face and half of his body from where he'd landed.

There were four crew members inside the troop compartment, faces covered with balaclavas. Three ignored the new passengers while the fourth helped them climb aboard and pointed to two seats. No sooner had the pilot entered behind them, than the hatch closed and Isnard felt the bird lift off.

The pilot made for the cockpit but Isnard grabbed him by the arm.

"What just happened?"

The pilot regarded the Marine for a moment. The spook wished he could see the man's eyes, tell what he was thinking. Finally the man responded.

"Not everyone in Afghanistan is *on the take*, as you Americans say. You have friends in high places, Mr. Isnard. It is lucky that they know who *their* friends are. I suggest you learn to do the same."

Without further explanation the pilot went to the cockpit. Isnard allowed the relief to flood his body like a much needed shower, cleansing, rejuvenating.

He sat down next to Andy who was getting an IV drip from the only crew member paying them any attention. A bag of fluid hung from a makeshift hook made from a bent coat hanger and three more sat in a crate on the floor.

He patted Andy on the cheek and received a weak smile in return. Andy's eyes were bloodshot and his eyelids kept drooping like he was going in and out of delirium.

"Close your eyes and get some rest," said Isnard, patting his own shoulder so that his friend would rest his head there.

Andy nodded and laid his head against his fellow Marine. He was snoring in less than a minute.

Isnard leaned his head back and exhaled. He hated to think what would've happened if he'd pulled the trigger. Thank God for small miracles.

* * *

KANDAHAR, AFGHANISTAN - 1:05AM AFT, AUGUST 25TH

They piled into Kreyling's two extended cab trucks, gear and one man in each of the beds. Daniel in one and Gaucho in the other.

No sooner had they left the airport compound than four sets of lights popped up behind them, maybe two hundred yards back, the gap closing quickly.

"You have a plan?" asked Cal.

"Sort of. I was more worried about getting you to the hangar. Didn't have much time to put a plan together," answered Kreyling who was driving. Rango was handling the second truck.

"Do you have some place we can go?"

"Sure, but I don't want to lead those bastards to find out where we stay. Let me give some old friends a call. They owe me."

Kreyling pulled out a cell phone and started giving clipped orders to the guy on the other line. It didn't sound like the Brit was talking to a friend, but that was just his way. All business. Niceties be damned.

Soon after he put the phone back in his pocket. "It's all set."

"What is?"

Kreyling's chuckle sounded more like a growl. "Don't bother your pretty little head about it, Yank. Her Majesty's finest have got you covered."

* * *

ANTHONY FARRAGO GRIPPED THE STEERING WHEEL WITH white knuckles, two of which still had blood on them from the beating he'd given the idiot in the tower. He'd never double-cross Farrago again.

His troops were gaining on the Americans and whoever had paid off the airport manager. Farrago couldn't wait to get his hands on them. He'd told his men that he didn't care if anyone on the other side came out alive, but he was now reconsidering the order. He had to find out what these newcomers knew and how they'd gotten in touch with Isnard.

The icing on the cake would be if they knew where Isnard and Andrews were. Sweeping up all the players in a neat little pile would not only save Farrago time, but it would allow him to green-light the rest of the operation. Time was ticking and he didn't have long. With Coles gently nudging from Washington, Farrago knew this was it for him. Fix things or find another job.

Hopefully after this one he wouldn't have to worry about his future. One way or another, Anthony Farrago was going to seal the deal and ensure his legacy. Most men would want to take a vacation after something like this. He was already thinking about the next chess match. For Farrago it was all about the chase, a fact that none of his wives had appreciated. Adrenaline fueled him, pushed him farther.

As he closed the gap with the two vehicles up ahead, Farrago thought of a line from one of his favorite movies, *Road House,* starring Patrick Swayze. Fitting for what he had planned coming from Sam Elliot's hard living character, Wade Garrett. *"I'll get all the sleep I need when I'm dead."* Farrago chuckled, popped another upper into his mouth, and pressed the pedal to the floor.

KANDAHAR, AFGHANISTAN

K reyling took a hard right, pulling into a small parking lot. Cal estimated twelve to fifteen parking spots marked by rubble and splashes of white spray paint. One story buildings surrounded the lot, making it sort of a court-yard. It looked like a death trap to Cal. Nowhere to go. Their pursuers were close.

"Please tell me you didn't take a wrong turn."

Kreyling just shook his head, snagged the shotgun off the dash and stepped out. Cal followed after motioning for Higgins and Neil Patel to stay in the truck.

He'd allow the Brit to lead whatever scheme he'd concocted, but he wouldn't risk his support personnel. Cal trusted the SAS veteran, his instincts in urban settings were uncanny. But sitting in an empty parking lot with no way out was crazy. At least they should take cover and setup a hasty ambush. Standing out in the open wasn't Cal's style.

Nope. Kreyling stood with his arms crossed facing the entrance, his face set with its usual grim determination.

The enemy approached, cautiously taking in the situation. Cal could only imagine what they were thinking. Good thing they didn't have mounted weapons.

They piled out all at once, black-clad stalkers wearing balaclavas. The two men heading toward Kreyling were not wearing masks, unperturbed by the lack of anonymity. A large Middle Easterner led the procession. He had one ear left and a jagged scar across his pock marked forehead that pushed his eyebrows down into an eternal scowl. He was not carrying a weapon that Cal could see.

The man just behind him had a lighter complexion and the facial features of a foreigner. He was smiling as if he'd just made a delicious discovery. Similar to his friend, this man's hands were empty.

The oversized ogre growled.

"Well you're one ugly bastard, aren't you?" said Kreyling, still maintaining his stance in front of Cal and the rest of the Americans. Rango lounged off to the side, running his hand back and forth along the length of his H&K.

Cal counted nineteen men, seventeen of whom were fanning out to cover any possible escape. The Marine glanced at Daniel Briggs who was casually taking in the display. He looked almost bored. MSgt Trent and Gaucho looked like they wanted to pounce, shifting their weight slowly from foot to foot.

Cal didn't doubt that his men could put up a good fight, but they were outnumbered. Casualties were inevitable. Not that he was scared of a fight, but better to wait for a more opportune moment.

The non-Arab pushed his goon aside and stepped forward.

"You're all under arrest."

"Under whose authority?" asked Kreyling.

"The Afghan government and The United States of America." An American. The guy had spook written all over him.

Kreyling chuckled. "Sorry, chap, but I don't take orders from you or your governments."

The man frowned. "And who do you take orders from?"

"Haven't you heard? I'm the Queen's butler. I go wherever the hell she tells me to go. Chamber pots are my specialty."

No one laughed. The tension and stakes were too high.

The stranger's mouth curved into a sarcastic smile. "My orders are to take you in. Someone will sort the rest out with your government later."

"Sorry. I've got my orders too, and they don't include sharing a cell with your overgrown ape," Kreyling said, motioning to the beast standing in front of him, whose eyes burned as he looked from target to target, obviously choosing his favorite one. He must have understood English because his head snapped back to Kreyling at the remark. He stepped forward, a drop of spittle leaking from his cracked lips.

Kreyling didn't move.

"I suggest you tell your foul friend to back away before I make him kiss the pavement," Kreyling said as if he'd asked for a napkin at the dinner table.

"I think I'd like to see that," said the spook.

A shrill whistle sounded from the closest rooftop. Cal's gaze followed the others. Barely visible all along the roof were more black clad shadows. They'd appeared all at once, completely silent. Cal's hand shifted on his weapon, readying for deployment. The look on the CIA guy's kept him from moving. Was it fear? Were those not his men on top of the buildings?

The answer came a moment later when Kreyling said, "As you can see, more of the Queen's staff have just arrived. I suggest you take your thugs and make for home. I wouldn't like to see what happens to you if you stick around."

The American looked from the newest arrivals to his own men. Some of his mercenaries were already backing away. They knew they were outnumbered, probably two to one.

"This isn't over. We'll see each other soon," the man said, locking his glare on Cal.

Cal grinned, lifted his hand and extended his middle finger.

The spook barked a command, and his minions slithered back into their vehicles and sped off into the night.

"I assume those are your friends?" Cal asked, pointing to the rooftops where the shadows were slipping down from their perches.

"Right. Some old SAS dogs and the odd Royal Marine. I think you'll like them."

Cal nodded. "I'd say I owe them a pint or two."

Kreyling's only visible eyebrow arched. "Don't let them hear that. They'll drink you broke if you let them."

Cal clapped his friend on the back and motioned for him to lead the way. He was looking forward to meeting Kreyling's friends.

* * *

1:39AM

The Hind touched down just outside of a small cluster of homes on the edge of Kandahar. Andy was on his third bag of IV fluids. The medic pulled out the IV line and moved on to securing his gear and opening the side hatch.

His face still covered, the pilot met them at the open door, a steady stream of desert sand blowing in from the prop wash. He put his mouth close to Isnard's ear.

"There is a man in that orchard," the pilot pointed into the inky blackness. "He will escort you the rest of the way."

"Thank you for helping us," said Isnard, for once at a loss for the right words.

The pilot nodded. "Do not give up on my country, Mr. Isnard. Despite what your papers might say, there are still those of us who believe in a free Afghanistan."

He shook Isnard's hand and returned to the cockpit. The medic waited for the Marines to debark. Isnard had to help Andy out, struggling to keep his friend upright. The fluids had brought color back to his face, but Andy still needed medical attention. His legs wobbled as he moved.

They ducked down as the helicopter rose into the air and flew north, the sound of its powerful engines fading into the blackness. Alone again.

They didn't move, letting their senses adjust to the darkness, taking in their new surroundings. A dog barked in the distance, followed by a car backfiring. Other than that the night was quiet, subdued.

When Isnard was confident that they weren't walking into an ambush, he eased Andy to his feet, and they made their way toward the walled orchard. They could only hope that this would be the last leg of their journey.

KANDAHAR, AFGHANISTAN

6:27AM AFT, AUGUST 25TH

Cal and his team said their goodbyes to the Brits who'd saved them five hours before. Over celebratory drinks, for which the former commandos kept a healthy stash in their posh accommodations, Cal learned that the British government was taking a more active role in the region. They were even calling in retired operators like the ones who'd come to Kreyling's call. According to one particularly crusty former Royal Marine colour sergeant, it was all because of the Zimmer Doctrine.

"I've gotta hand it to your president," he'd said. "Took a lot of balls to stand up there and say what he did. Good to know you boys are back in the fight."

There was a level of excitement in the air that Cal hadn't felt since just after 9-11. The troops were restless, like baying hounds pulling at their master's leash. These men had spent their entire adult lives training for war. It was all they knew. Some were married with families, others were terminal bachelors. But together they were family.

The Jefferson Group men fit right in with their cousins from across the sea, trading stories and swapping ribbing between men of battle. It was obvious to Cal that Kreyling had passed the word: "These Americans are with me."

Cal watched their interaction, how Kreyling never filled his own beer or how conversations quieted when he came near. His countrymen looked to the one-eyed warrior with something like awe. He was a legend. There were the whispered tales of top secret raids and black ops takedowns. Kreyling was THE hero eclipsing the rest.

As The Jefferson Group team poured out into the dawn, Dr. Higgins asked to speak with Cal. The normally outgoing doctor had kept to himself since their run-in with the CIA.

"What's on your mind, Doc?"

Higgins rubbed his left temple and took off his glasses, polishing them on the sleeve of his shirt.

"I'm sorry it's taken me this long, but I think I know who that man was."

Bingo. "The spook?"

Higgins nodded, replacing his glasses in their original position. "If I am correct, I'm eighty-five percent sure by the way, I could only just make out his face, the man's name is Anthony Farrago. I never had direct dealings with the man, but from what I remember he may be somewhat of a challenge."

"Why?"

"There was an instance involving a colleague who oversaw the periodic mental evaluations of field agents. He came to me one day needing a second opinion. It involved this man Farrago.

"At the time Farrago was something of a wunderkind, a natural. He'd had great success and was seen as part of the Agency's future. He had all the attributes of a career agent, a living double-oh-seven."

"Then why did your colleague bring it to you?"

"At first glance I wondered the same thing. He did not explain his concern, but suggested that I take the file and examine it when I had time, said he did not want to taint my opinion. It was not an uncommon request, so of course I said I would look at it. Because he said it was not pressing, it took me a few days to get to it. When I did, I read it over four or five times, seeing nothing out of the ordinary, nothing that would make me doubt Farrago's abilities. I even looked at his confidential operational file and everything looked routine, if not exceptional.

"Then I found the thread. Sometimes we miss things because they are so normal, little bits that we typically take for granted. What I found was that although his tests all came back swimmingly, when you compared the separate reports they didn't match up."

Cal shook his head. "I think you lost me."

Higgins grunted then started again. "Have you ever taken a personality test, one that tells you what your natural tendencies are?"

"You mean like the alphabet tests, Myers-Briggs, or DISC?"

"Exactly. The main difference being that the CIA builds its own, changing them frequently. In fact, I was one of the Agency's question formulators. Fascinating work really. Anyhow, from what I remember, Farrago's tests all came back positive, no anomalies. But when I compared one exam to another, I noticed that there were slight variations. Looked at independently, even a keen eye would've categorized them as two different people. It all started to make sense, including the reason why my colleague brought the file to my attention."

"You lost me again, Doc. What's so bad about that? Those

tests aren't one hundred percent accurate are they? I've never seen an eval that is."

"Of course not. No test is infallible. There is always a certain margin of error. But let me ask you a question. Have you ever had someone under your command that you knew deep down, but could never prove, was lying or telling only part of the truth?"

"Sure. But doesn't the CIA train their agents to lie?"

"Yes, but the testing usually circumvents that tendency. I have only seen it a handful of times in my career, but Farrago fell into the outlier category. There are pathological liars, and then there are those who believe an alternate reality. Each of the two types have a proclivity for manipulating interrogations and lie detector tests. When I again consulted with my colleague, we concluded that Farrago fell into an even smaller category. He exhibited characteristics of both the pathological liar and the delusional."

"So you're saying that not only was he crazy, but he was sane enough to lie about it?" asked Cal, still struggling with what Higgins was implying.

"You know how I feel about the word crazy, Calvin, but yes that's about it in a nutshell."

"What did you do with the report?"

"There wasn't much we could do without concrete evidence. This was more of a hunch. We made a note that was essentially a recommendation to keep an eye on Farrago for certain indicators, and to reevaluate should that happen."

"And did it?"

"I don't know. I left shortly after that to work for SSI."

"So tell me what we're dealing with, Doc, in layman's terms."

Higgins nodded, taking a second to gather his thoughts. "Farrago will be like a chameleon, blending in as he needs. His words weave at the whim of his fancy, probably to his own benefit. If he believes something is right, he will put all effort into it, rarely straying from that path. He is cunning, intelligent, and highly manipulative."

Cal didn't like the sound of that. He'd dealt with all sorts of enemies and he liked the smart ones the least.

"So how do I explain this to the rest of the guys? Can you give me an example that I can use?"

Higgins frowned. "That's an easy one. Take your pick: Mao, Hitler, Stalin. All the deadliest dictators in history generally fall into the same category. Men who believe that their reality, their way, is the only way. *That* is what we are dealing with."

WASHINGTON, D.C

Due to the time change, it was still the previous night on the East Coast. The nation's capital settled in for the night, tucking in after another muggy late summer day. Travis Haden was still hours away from going to bed. Another all-nighter loomed.

He'd just talked to Cal, his cousin filling him in on the last twenty-four hours of mayhem. The thing that worried both cousins the most was the CIA's involvement. How had they known about Cal's team heading to Kandahar? What was this Farrago character after and who was he working for?

The hard part was figuring out how to deal with the situation in a decisive manner. Travis's SEAL mentality wanted to attack. But any action on his part would tell the culprits that the president and his chief of staff were privy to the covert operation. One of Travis's most important functions was to shield his boss from scandal. This operation had the ability to blow things sky high.

He had buddies from his Navy days who were now at

Langley. They could be trusted, but were they being watched?
Travis decided to take the chance. He needed answers.

AN HOUR LATER, TRAVIS WAS PICKING AT A PILE OF SLOPPY
fries at *The Saloon* on U Street Northwest. He'd come to love
the little bar. It had been the sign out front that had pulled
him in months earlier while he was out for a late night jog:

The Saloon
Est. 1977
A Quiet Neighborhood Pub
NO T.V.
NO Standing
NO American Express
NO Martinis
NO Cigars
NO Shots
NO Pretending

Aside from the sign, he'd taken to the place immediately.
As advertised, the pub felt like a trip back to the seventies.
The ever-present smell of decades of Belgian beer and simple
pub food. Cheerful staff and clientele. It was like an old
leather chair that welcomed you into its embrace on a cold
winter day. It was also a perfect place to hunker down, have a
beer and be left alone.

Roger Horn walked in ten minutes after Travis, ordering a
beer on the way in without making eye contact with his old
friend. By the time he made it through the bustling crowd he
was halfway through his pint. Roger wasn't much to look at.
Thin to the point of being bony, with wiry arms; more than
one operator had thought that meant the man was weak. His

droopy eyes looked like something out of a old gangster movie, the languid mob enforcer.

They'd gone through Basic Underwater Demolition/Seal (BUD/S) training together, Travis the newbie lieutenant and Roger the level-headed non-commissioned officer. Most people didn't think much of Roger Horn when they first met him. Travis hadn't.

But Roger was one tough S.O.B. He never complained, even when he'd broken his back on a night drop over Taiwan. He'd passed out in Travis's arms. His career with the SEALs was over after that. Now he was a CIA analyst.

They got together whenever Travis had time, which wasn't much considering his new job.

"What are you drinking?" Roger asked, downing the rest of his midnight ale.

"Lager."

"Pussy," Roger said, already waving for another drink. The pretty bartender nodded her understanding. "How are things in the castle on the hill?"

Travis shrugged. "Busy, but what else is new?"

"Looks like Zimmer's coming around. He's got Langley scrambling to do a new character assessment."

"He's a good guy. I wouldn't have taken the job if I didn't think he could do his."

The bartender delivered Roger's beer and pointed to Travis's half-full glass.

"I'm good thanks."

Travis waited until she was out of earshot, then asked. "You still got friends in operations?"

Roger nodded.

"You know a guy by the name of Farrago?"

Roger set his beer down.

"Yeah. I know Farrago."

Roger's tone expressed his opinion of Farrago loud and clear. *Danger*.

"What does he do for the Agency?"

Roger took another swig of beer. "Farrago works for the deputy director NCS."

"Kingsley Coles?" Travis blurted. If Farrago was linked to Coles, things were about to go from bad to worse.

"Yeah. How do you know him?"

"I met him the other day."

"What did you think?"

This was Roger's style. He wasn't going to give Travis anything before he knew what his old team leader had in his pocket.

"Reminded me of a stuck up trust fund baby with a dirt phobia."

Roger chuckled. "It's called mysophobia, by the way, the dirt phobia, but that's not totally accurate. Obsessive compulsive, yes. I would've said aloof too, but people say that about me."

That was true. Roger had a way of making people think that he didn't care. Nothing could be farther from the truth, it was just that he was very good at hiding his emotions.

"What does Farrago do for Coles?"

"I think he's listed as an assistant or deputy, but he's really a cleanup man, a utility guy for whatever Coles needs."

"Do you know him?"

Roger shook his head. "I've seen him a couple times, but he doesn't spend much time in Langley anymore. Whispers say he hangs out in the desert kingdoms."

If Farrago worked for Coles, that meant that Coles knew what his man was doing. Did that mean that the director of the CIA knew too? If so, getting Andy and Isnard back on U.S. soil would prove challenging.

"Is there any way you can find out what he's doing right now?"

"Can I ask why?"

"I don't think you want to know."

"If I'm going to go snooping around in spook-land, it sure as hell would make it easier if I knew why I was looking."

Travis didn't want to get Roger in trouble. Maybe he should find another avenue to get the information he needed. But his options were limited, nonexistent actually aside from Roger Horn.

"Look, I don't want you going to Leavenworth for this."

"They don't send Agency employees to Leavenworth."

"You know what I mean."

Roger shrugged and motioned for Travis to continue.

"I've got some friends in Afghanistan who just had a run-in with Farrago. We don't know how he found out or why he tried to arrest them."

"Are you telling me that Farrago *didn't* nab your friends?" Roger asked, his tone incredulous.

"Like I said, he tried."

Roger whistled softly. "I tip my hat to your friends, but they better watch their backs. You piss off a guy like Farrago and you end up with a bullet in your head."

"Does that mean you won't look into it?"

Roger grinned. It was the same look he gave then Lieutenant Travis Haden every time they were about to do something stupid.

"It's been pretty slow this week. It'll give me something to do."

They shared another round and left separately. Travis watched his old comrade stroll down U Street, a slight hitch in his step from his spinal injury. Most guys would've taken the disability and lived the rest of their lives on vacation, but not Roger Horn. Despite what the doctors had said, he'd regained the use of his legs and was almost allowed to return to his SEAL team. Almost. You can only hide a limp for so long.

Travis admired the hell out of him for that and many other things. Hopefully he could use that old toughness and find out something that Travis could pass on to Cal. His gut told the former SEAL that things were about to get worse. What he wouldn't give to be in Kandahar with Cal at that very moment, a gun instead of a pen in his hand.

KANDAHAR, AFGHANISTAN

7:14AM AFT, AUGUST 25TH

Andy barely remembered the meandering trip through the city. Floating in and out of consciousness, the Marine only saw flitting images as they bounced along in the back of the ancient Volkswagen Beetle. No front or back bumpers. The exhaust fumes poured in making him even more nauseous as he tried to sleep. The driver, whom they'd met in the orchard, insisted on waiting until daylight to move from the hidden location.

Andy vaguely remembered Isnard arguing with the man, pressing him to leave sooner. But the man wouldn't budge, saying that they'd be safer as one of thousands in the swarm of morning Kandahar traffic.

He was right, but the incessant honks and jostling only added to Andy's discomfort. Instead of stopping, he threw up into a shallow metal bucket. Not that he had anything left in his stomach, but the man driving didn't want bile stains in his sputtering baby. The thing smelled like a century's worth of stale cigarette smoke and body odor. Another wonderful addition to Andy's already overwhelmed senses.

He'd lost all track of time, sometimes hearing Rich Isnard's voice, sometimes not. Andy had been wounded before, shot, almost blown up, but the gut-wrenching weakness was driving him mad. He'd never felt so helpless. It wasn't his body. He couldn't focus on anything, so he took to pinching his upper thigh, as if the gesture would keep him grounded. Reality corralled for another moment.

After what seemed like hours of driving, the old car putted into a walled complex, rocking from side to side as it rolled over a homemade speed bump. Andy registered the presence of guards, both armed, unsmiling as the car made its way in.

Isnard shook his arm. "Hey, we're here."

Andy nodded and tried to pull himself upright. His hand shook and it started a chain reaction down his arm and across his shoulders. He almost passed out.

"Let me help you," said Isnard. He slipped out of the vehicle and hurried around to Andy's side. With one arm over his friend, Andy shuffled along, willing his body to comply. He made it five steps (he knew because he counted each one) before his legs gave out and his vision shifted, white faded to nothing.

* * *

THE GUARDS AND THE DRIVER WEREN'T GOING TO BE ANY help. Isnard heaved Andy across his shoulders in a fireman's carry and followed their guide into the modest home. He could smell the pungent herbs of someone's breakfast as he stepped across the threshold. His stomach growled as they moved through the main living area, down a narrow hallway and into a courtyard.

A concrete fountain tinkled in the corner, water rushing over a crude landscape that was washing away daily, its once etched facade now smoothed and slick. An umbrella was propped in the corner, under which sat a man reading a book. He looked up, setting the book in his lap.

Isnard was short, but this guy was shorter, probably barely breaking five feet. He had close cropped white hair and a deep tan. Under a flowing white shirt and matching linen pants, Isnard could tell that the man's build was slight, but his forearms were wiry strong. His face looked vaguely familiar, but then again, members of separate races always said that about the others. Rich had been in the Middle East for most of his career and he'd still have a hard time giving an accurate description of anyone of Arab descent to a sketch artist.

The man nodded to the driver who almost bowed down to the floor.

"Thank you for your service. You may go," said the man.

The driver didn't hesitate, backing away as if he was leaving the presence of a demigod.

"How is your friend?" the man asked in English, his accent deep and laced with formality of a British nobleman.

"Not so hot. You wouldn't happen to have a physician on-call would you?"

The man pulled a cell phone out of his pocket and tapped away like an American teenager whose only focus was video games. Who was this guy?

Andy was getting heavier. Rich shifted him a bit to the left, not wanting to interrupt their host. Sweat dripping down his back.

The man replaced the phone in his pocket and regarded his guest. "My physician will be here soon. Why don't we take your friend inside. Please, follow me."

AN HOUR LATER, ANDY WAS A QUARTER OF THE WAY through his second bag of IV fluid. Much needed water and electrolytes pumped into the unconscious Marine's body, working their soothing magic. The doctor was quiet as he worked, showing extreme deference to the man in white who'd disappeared shortly after the doctor arrived, promising to return soon.

"Your friend is quite dehydrated and seems to have contracted Hepatitis. Hepatitis A is common in the region, and he exhibits the symptoms. Giardia is also a possibility depending on where he has been. Fluids and rest should help. Antibiotics and further medication will be needed, things I do not have. I would recommend a hospital stay if possible." The doctor's accent was similar to the man in white. Professional. Precise. Even aristocratic.

"I don't think that's gonna be possible," said Isnard. "How soon can he move?"

Isnard thought the doctor was going to demand further medical attention, but instead he shrugged as if he was used to having his professional diagnoses ignored.

"Whenever you'd like. I would recommend he gets his fill of fluids first. The anti-nausea medication I injected should also help. Simple Tylenol will lower his fever. These things take time. Get him somewhere to recuperate, give his body a chance to heal."

The doctor pointed to Isnard's arm.

"Would you like me to look at that?"

The Baghdad station chief looked down at his arm. He hadn't even noticed the blood on his sleeve and the gash underneath. It must've happened when they'd run from the tribal camp. The wound stung but didn't really hurt.

"Sure. Thanks, doctor."

The physician nodded and inspected the wound. Mending it as he had with hundreds or thousands before. He even convinced Isnard to sit down and have his own IV line inserted. Two bags later, the Marine felt like a new man. All he needed now was some food and a shower.

As the doctor extracted the needle from his arm, the man in white reappeared. He was smiling like he'd just taken a leisurely stroll through the park. A man totally at peace in the world. He reminded Isnard of the Buddhist monks he'd seen during a backpacking trip through Nepal.

"I think it is time for you to make a phone call," the man said, handing Isnard a phone that still had the plastic sticky wrapper on its screen.

"Who do you want me to call?" Isnard asked. He didn't know where he was or who he was dealing with. His gut told him the man meant them no harm, but maybe that was just the hope tingling in his chest.

"Call your American friends. They arrived last night. We have much to discuss."

It took him a second to understand who the guy was talking about. Cal Stokes? How did he know?

"I'm not sure who you mean," replied Isnard, still wary of the man's intent.

"I was told that Calvin Stokes Junior landed in a Gulf-stream G650ER at approximately twelve thirty five this morning. They were pursued by another force, but were able to avoid capture with the help of some British friends. Mr. Stokes is now staying in a secure location not ten minutes drive from here."

The blunt recital was like a punch in the stomach. How did this guy know so much? Who tried to apprehend Cal and who were the Brits that helped? There were too many questions to ask, but Isnard had one that had to be answered first.

"I'm sorry, I guess I never introduced..."

"I know who you are Mr. Isnard. Former Marine and now former Baghdad station chief for the CIA."

The surprise hit him again, like a sledge hammer this time at the mention of him being the "former" station chief in Baghdad. He wasn't used to being on the receiving end of unexpected news..

"And who, may I ask, do I have the pleasure of speaking with, sir?"

The man bowed at the waist, formally, like he was greeting a head of state.

"My name is Kadar Saladin. I believe you have already met my brother."

KANDAHAR, AFGHANISTAN

9:49AM AFT, AUGUST 25TH

His senses returned gradually. The smell of cheap concrete construction. The touch of a thin wool blanket on his finger. Light streaming in from a part in the curtains that made him squint and look away.

When he did turn his head, Andy almost jumped at the realization that someone, no not someone, multiple some-ones were looking down at him. He could see their outlines, blurry blobs.

He heard a car door slamming shut.

"How you feeling, Marine?" came the question piercing his muffled hearing. Familiar.

"Cal?"

"Yeah. I've got Top, Daniel and some of the others boys with me too."

It took massive effort for the normally composed Marine major to not give in to his feelings. The level of relief he felt surprised him. The gushing emotion of being reunited with comrades, knowing that no matter what happened next he wouldn't be alone.

"When...how..." he croaked.

"We got here a few minutes ago. Why don't you rest up and we'll..."

Before Andy knew what he was doing, his hand grabbed Cal's arm, pulling him closer, suddenly desperate.

"Don't go...have to tell you..."

Cal patted Andy's hand. "It's okay, we're not going anywhere. We'll have plenty of time to talk later. We're safe here."

Andy's body sagged back against the mattress, weary relief fogging his senses once again. Something told him that it was probably the drugs they'd given him, or maybe the realization that someone had his back. It was the last thought he had before he slipped back to his dreams.

* * *

CAL HELD HIS FRIEND'S HAND FOR A MOMENT LONGER, NOT wanting to wake him. Andy hadn't been imprisoned long, but the lack of proper nutrition coupled with the stress and whatever bacteria he had running through his veins had taken its toll. Dark circles ringed Andy's eyes, the sickly mustard and slate color clung to his face. He needed a shave and a few hot showers.

He set Andy's hand back on the bed and stood, looking to his friends who'd said nothing, reverently watching the interaction.

"Let's talk to Isnard. I want to find out who did this to him."

* * *

FOR SOME REASON, ANTHONY FARRAGO'S TEMPER HELD. He knew what his boss would say before placing the call. Kingsley Coles had not been happy. Stokes and his men were supposed to be in custody, out of the way.

It wasn't that Farrago couldn't take an ass-chewing. Far from it. But screaming wasn't Coles's style. He'd evenly reiterated Farrago's mission and simply said, "Last chance, Mr. Farrago."

Like a worker bee whose only motivation was a looming deadline, the pressure fed Farrago's fire. His mind spun in asymmetric angles, analyzing and reanalyzing his options. He would've made a helluva card shark if he'd had the inclination. Counting cards and stacking decks was child's play. He excelled at juggling twenty balls in the air, nary a one falling to the ground.

But now there was a ball threatening to fall from his carefully orchestrated act. In the grand scheme of things, the newest players were a minor inconvenience. There were much bigger things on the horizon that anything less than a full court press by the American government could not stop. The wave was coming and Farrago planned on surfing it into the sunset. Time to get back to work.

* * *

1:21PM

Andy woke to an empty room, the IV in his arm no longer there. While he felt far from his best, he felt a helluva lot better than when he'd stumbled into his temporary residence.

It didn't take him long to find the others. He followed the voices until he entered a large living space, weathered sofas arranged in a circle. His friends were there, Cal, MSgt Willy Trent, Rich Isnard, Gaucho, and Daniel Briggs. Even Neil

Patel and Dr. Higgins were in attendance, a fact that surprised him. Was this all for him?

Andy didn't recognize all the faces, but his eyes locked on a single man, a stranger in white attire. The Arab sat crossed legged like a holy man, his small frame easily fitting in the canvas love seat.

He addressed the others in a level tone, like a patient teacher. The man looked up when Andy stepped into the room.

"Welcome, Major Andrews."

Andy nodded to the man and the others turned.

The giant MSgt Trent was the first to hop up from his seat.

"Here, take mine," he said.

Trent patted him on the back as he took his seat. Again the welling of emotion, like he'd escaped the jaws of death and somehow landed back home, amongst his fellow Marines.

"Should I begin my tale again?" the man in white asked Cal.

"If you wouldn't mind," replied Cal.

The man nodded, pausing to take a careful sip of his tea. Then, when everyone had settled in, the man in white began.

"Major Andrews, my name is Kadar Saladin. You had the pleasure of meeting my youngest brother Latif in Gereshk."

Andy had almost forgotten about the merchant. The last time he'd seen the man was after they'd hopped on the nomad's tanks and left the broken checkpoint.

"Is he okay?" asked Andy.

"He is," said Kadar, solemnly. "Many were killed in the helicopter attack, but my brother is well. He has always had a gift for walking away relatively unscathed. His mother, my step-mother, used to say he was blessed by Allah with the ability to walk between rain drops. That is Latif."

He took another sip of his tea and continued.

"Now, for the history of my family..."

THE LINEAGE OF THE SALADIN CLAN STRETCHED BACK centuries. Its earliest known ancestors spawned from the ranks of the great Saladin who'd warded off the western Crusaders in the 12th century. A fierce warrior tested in battle and gifted in rule, Saladin later became the first Sultan of Egypt and Syria. With his power he formed the Ayyubid Dynasty.

Somewhere along the way, a handful of his men began to take his name for their own, honoring their lord by using the surname al-Saladin. Upon his death in 1193, much of Saladin's wealth went to his most loyal subjects. The majority of this core group of Saladin's men went their separate ways. Some enjoyed their amassed fortunes in Damascus, others retired to a quieter life in the country and others sought more.

Kadar Saladin's earliest known ancestor was a fierce warrior known as The Scourge of Hattin, for his valorous actions during the defeat of the Crusaders at the battle of Hattin. The victory served as a tipping point for the renewal of Muslim power in the region and was followed by the recapture of Palestine soon after.

Kadar's ancestor left Saladin's capital of Damascus and travelled back to his homeland, what was now known as modern Afghanistan. Family lore said that the warrior searched for a new calling, never quite turning his back on his past.

He settled on a large estate he'd purchased, his brood of somewhere over thirty children and countless retinue in tow. Alone with his thoughts, the warrior pondered his fading future. He was no longer a young man, his bones growing frail, the muscles on his large frame tight. And yet he yearned for a legacy, something he could leave for his children and his children's children. Riches were not enough. They could be spent in a summer. Deeds on the battlefield passed from memory. No, his family needed more.

According to Kadar, he found the seed one day as he walked through one of his olive plantations, touring the land with the proprietor. Somewhere in the middle of the conversation, a group of three men approached, demanding information from the plantation manager, even threatening death should he refuse their request. They were brazen men with the swagger of cutthroats.

Before the man could answer, Kadar's ancestor cut in, acting the part of a humble servant, a loyal underling of his rich master.

"What information would you like, my lords?" he asked.

Much to his surprise, the men wanted to know about him, The Scourge of Hattin. There were wild rumors of his extravagant wealth, mounds of gold and pillars made of diamond, and these men were hellbent on obtaining their share. They bragged of having a troop of over one hundred men who could take the land and spoils if needed.

While Kadar's ancestor doubted their boasts, he decided to see where the adventure would lead. It had been too long since he'd felt the tingle of battle, the taste of blood on his curved sword. Even at his advanced age, he could have taken all three men single-handedly, but he held back, bowing in deference, telling them anything they wanted to know.

The men left in barely concealed glee. Kadar's ancestor saw the greed in their eyes. They would act soon, and his heart beat a tiny bit faster at the thought.

When he returned to his estate, he gathered his eldest sons, those whom he'd trained to be his advisors, his personal guard, strapping young men with sharp minds just like their father. He often quizzed them about the wisdom of this or that action, always preaching the way of the cunning yet honorable warrior.

The sons listened to their father's tale, more than one probably asking for their patron's permission to find the rascals and kill them outright. The Scourge of Hattin merely smiled, calming his sons as he'd calmed his men before storming the walled cities of the Crusaders.

He outlined his plan, making each son promise that not a hair on a single attacker's head be harmed. He never said why, but insisted that there would be a grand lesson at the end.

It wasn't two days later that the rogues made their play, marching right down the wide dirt path that led to the entrance of his estate. There weren't one hundred men in the ragtag band, it was closer to twenty.

Appearing as if out of thin air, his sons descended with their own men, bows strung, blades ready for slaughter. The overwhelming force surrounded the men at the gate, daring the intruders to act. Weapons dropped to the ground as the smaller group realized their folly. Not one was harmed as the three men who'd visited the olive plantation were now escorted to the man they'd come to steal from, The Scourge of Hattin.

He listened to their pleas, nodding at their apologies, even offering them food and drink. Their groveling stopped and his questions began.

They told him that they were part of a larger network of spies and mercenaries who lorded over much of ancient Afghanistan. They told him who the key leaders were, who had the power, where they lived. After half a day of questioning, the father had had enough.

He said his goodbyes to the three men, wishing them a safe journey. Then he quietly ordered his sons to kill the men and dispose of their bodies. His orders were followed, and

The Scourge of Hattin retreated to his private chambers for seven days.

When he finally emerged, he laid out the plans for his family. He'd seen the vital importance of information as he'd served his own glorious master, the great Saladin. Without good intelligence they never would have known how many men they were attacking or where the best route would be. Good men with superior intelligence could conquer a superior force nine times out of ten.

And so Kadar's ancestor methodically set out to take over the network of spies and mercenaries in the region. It did not happen overnight, and there was some bloodshed, but by the time of his death, the Saladin legacy was set, strong enough to weather the ravages of passing centuries.

"THERE HAVE BEEN MANY INVADERS OVER THE YEARS. THE Soviets, the British, the Taliban and even you Americans. Along the way my family has stayed in the shadows, fostering my ancestor's legacy. We do not always ally with the right side, but we try our best, always seeking that which is honorable.

"As a young man, I followed my father as he rode our best horses along the twisting paths of the Afghan mountains wielding Stinger missiles provided by the American government. I am also proud to call your former Congressman Charlie Wilson a friend and a fellow warrior."

Andy knew all about Congressman Charlie Wilson. Hollywood had even made a movie based on a book written about Wilson's Afghanistan quest in the 1980's called *Charlie Wilson's War: The Extraordinary Story of the Largest Covert Operation in History*. The Texas Democrat was a legend for what he'd done to supply the Afghan Mujahideen with weapons during the Soviet incursion.

"I saved Charlie's life one day from assassination, and he reciprocated soon after, catching my arm as my horse took a rare misstep and knocked me from the saddle, almost off a sheer cliff face. We kept in touch for many years. He helped strengthen my family's ties with your best operatives. I was very sorry to hear of his death."

Kadar bowed his head, closing his eyes, probably saying a silent prayer for the American cowboy. Andy could just imagine the larger-than-life Rep. Charlie Wilson standing next to the diminutive Kadar Saladin.

"Now I am the leader of my family, the humble leader of a vast network run by my father and his father before him. To my knowledge we are the longest standing intelligence network in the known world."

"I still don't understand how you found us, how you knew about Andy," said Cal, the distrust plain in his voice. Andy knew Cal, understood that his friend had listened to Kadar's tale, but it didn't mean he'd trust the man. "Do you work for the CIA?" It was an accusation more than a question.

Kadar returned Cal's stare. Calm. Serene. Andy knew that this man was not used to being questioned. He ruled by blood right and probably by deed. If he'd been on the front lines against the Soviets, he'd more than likely fought against the Taliban too. He was not a man to be taken lightly. But could he trusted?

As if reading Andy's mind, Kadar said, "You do not trust me Mr. Stokes, and that is good. You and I live in a world of shadows, where one wrong move spells doom. I do not work for the CIA. We have been known to lend them our expertise, but we are not held under their thumb. No, much like you, I have friends in your government. They have pledged themselves to me and I to them. We understand the world as it is, full of cruel men who would seek to grind the rest of us to dust. There are such men in your government as well here in my country. We meet here today because those forces will converge, and soon."

Cal spoke up again. "I appreciate everything, really I do. You've rescued one of my best friends and given us a place to stay. My next priority is getting us on a plane and back home."

"I am afraid that is not possible," said Kadar.

"I'm sorry?" said Cal, his tone sharp. "No offense, but for us it's mission accomplished. I'd be happy to compensate you if you'd like, but we have more pressing matters in America."

Kadar shook his head, his face grave. "I am afraid you misunderstand me, Mr. Stokes. You are free to leave whenever you like. I cannot keep you here. But I believe it would be in your best interest to stay in Afghanistan and help me do what I plan to do."

"And what is that?"

"I am honor-bound to kill the man who has stolen billions of dollars from my country, and who will soon run away with much more, leaving our government and people in broken ruins."

Cal shook his head as if trying to understand. "Wait, who are you talking about?"

Before Kadar could answer, Andy said, "The President of Afghanistan, Cal."

KABUL, AFGHANISTAN

11:03AM AFT, AUGUST 25TH

The President of Afghanistan watched as the organized chaos swirled around him. Staff and movers tried to shuffle around his office in a respectful way, but the odd thump from a moving cabinet or scrape from a dislodged picture frame inevitably elicited a grunt from behind the ornate carved desk.

September 2nd was the deadline. He'd told both presidential candidates, in an effort to move the contentious elections along, that he would leave on that day. It was up to them to do the rest. He'd done enough. Survived assassination attempts. Dealt with warring tribal leaders. Brokered economic stimulus packages with foreign powers, essentially groveled at the feet of the world.

He was already a wealthy man, his worth officially reported in the millions. Not a small sum for a man of his background. In 2002, he never would have dreamed where the war might lead. Before the American invasion, Afghanistan was ruled by the squeezing noose of the Taliban.

Their ouster was quick and the flow of aid came soon after. Many Afghans had better lives because of it, but much had simply reverted back to old ways. Tribal lines redrawn or bolstered, ancient rivalries renewed.

Most thought he'd done a good job as leader of the war-torn nation. He thought so. Twelve years in office. Thousands and thousands of miles traveled. Countless contacts made.

But retirement beckoned. As a gift from the people, he'd received an estate and servants, a parting thank-you for all that he had done. He didn't plan on living there long, if at all. Over the preceding decade, billions of dollars flowed into his country. A good portion went to the people, to school construction, and the payment of poppy farmers to no longer harvest their crop for heroin. It was impossible to keep tabs on where every penny went, and that was a good thing.

The naive citizens of first world countries believed their money was being well spent, accounted for and fully recorded. That was not how things worked. World leaders knew that. Intelligence agencies used it to their advantage, as did politicians and multinational corporations.

The President of Afghanistan did not consider himself a greedy man, but he did feel that he deserved his fair share for the danger he'd withstood and the time he'd spent traveling the globe for the benefit of his countrymen. He told himself that what he was taking was but a pittance compared to the whole.

And so for six years he and an intimate group of advisors had designed a system to shuffle and funnel funds. Shell corporations. Road projects with ridiculously high margins. Payment to warlords with guaranteed kickbacks. And behind it all was the face of Afghanistan, the brave leader who'd stood up for his people, worked tirelessly for their well-being.

He'd learned a good deal from his time with companies like Shell and GE, companies who wanted to invest in

Afghanistan. Not only had he taken their money, he also took their knowledge.

He was fascinated to learn that IBM had started as a computer company and was now one of the leading consultancies in the world. They'd learned from their own trial and error, built a system, and then taught it to others who wanted the same success. That was exactly what he wanted.

He was too young to retire, his energy still high despite the sweat and tears shed over the last twelve years. A brief respite yes, but there was a system to sell, his system, and there were those in the world who would pay handsomely for it.

* * *

KANDAHAR, AFGHANISTAN - 12:41PM AFT

The raid force swept into the compound. Kadar Saladin had known the exact location. He'd confirmed the number of inhabitants. Nineteen.

Daniel Briggs led the way, Cal right behind. No sounds in the house, dishes littering the dining room table. Scraps and garbage all over the kitchen. Farther they went, deeper into the two story building. Weapons ready, moving left and right, hand signals pointing and motioning with practiced ease.

The stairs were steep. A perfect ambush point. A couple grenades dropped down and they were toast. Cal's heart pounded, his eyes darting from corner to corner.

They'd taken down the gate guards easily, expecting more inside. No one so far.

Higher they climbed. Narrow hallway above. MSgt Trent and Gaucho were right behind. Kreyling's countrymen had volunteered to come along. They secured the perimeter, sweeping up behind them. The only thing to sweep up so far was crumbs and trash.

Cal wanted in first. No one objected, except for Daniel, of course. He always took point.

Smooth steps, dirty laundry thrown outside bedrooms. Cal smelled the iron odor of men sharing a house together, too many for one this size.

Still no sounds excepted for the brush of an arm behind him, or the muffled clank of their weapons. Water dripped from some unseen faucet ahead, irregular in its cadence.

They stacked outside the first bedroom, the door hanging open, only darkness inside. Blackout curtains closed. *One, two, three.*

No flash bangs, just in case. They flooded the room, switching on rail mounted red lights as they entered.

There were three sets of bunk beds shoved against opposite walls. Six beds total. Mounds in each one. Daniel nudged one with his hand. No movement.

Cal flipped his light from red to white, bathing the sleeping man with LED glare. The dark stain ran from the man's head and onto the mattress, crimson and brown dripping onto the bed below.

Room to room they went. They found the same scene in each one. The hulking brute from the confrontation with Farrago was in the last room, a single.

Eighteen men dead, clean kills, and no sign of Anthony Farrago.

They headed downstairs after a quick search for anything that would point to where their enemy had gone. Nothing.

When they got back to the front of the house, Kreyling reported that his men hadn't found anything. Farrago had somehow killed every one of his men and slipped away. Maybe Kadar Saladin could find out where he'd gone.

As they exited the front door, Cal scanned what he could

see of the horizon. The sun was directly overhead, its rays relentlessly oppressive. He heard a strange humming. Cal turned, trying to see where it was coming from. The proximity of the walled homes made it hard to pinpoint the source of the sound. Then, one hundred yards away, he saw three small shapes pop into view.

Cal cupped his free hand over his eyes and squinted. The objects were coming closer, the buzzing getting louder. They looked like strange birds. Not birds, remote controlled drones with spinning rotors propelling them closer.

Cal lifted his weapon and fired a three round burst. Amazingly the drones scattered. He'd missed but now everyone in the raid force was firing. One went down. A rotor burst on a second, the thing sputtering slower but still crept along.

The third acted, followed a split second later by the damaged drone. In total eight tiny rockets launched, suddenly outdistancing the mother birds, reaching out for their targets below.

There wasn't anything else for Cal and his men to do but turn and run.

* * *

KABUL, AFGHANISTAN - 12:45PM

A knock came from the blank wall behind him, a secret entrance.

"Will you please excuse me," the Afghan president said to the staff who were shuttling and packing. No one said a word, just left what they were doing and closed the door behind them.

The knock came again. The president pushed his lunch plate away and rapped three times on his desk. Without a sound the secret entrance swiveled open.

"Tony. It is good to see you my friend," the Afghan president stood and embraced the American.

Anthony Farrago returned the embrace with one arm, the other hand holding a black duffle bag.

"It's good to see you again, Mr. President."

"You will not be calling me that for long."

"Do you think those idiots will figure it out before the deadline?"

The president shrugged. "They do not have a choice. I am leaving."

Tony nodded and set the bag down next to the desk. Neither man acknowledged it. The Afghan had made it plain that he despised such crude gestures. It was his traveling money and nothing else. Not a bribe. A small sum compared to what they'd been able to sock away in various overseas accounts. Even tinier than what he would soon inherit. He'd have to remind the American not to bring money with him again. Bribes were reserved for thieves and simpletons.

They sat in the last two chairs left in his office, the flag of Afghanistan staring down at them.

The President of Afghanistan cracked open a gold pocket case (a present from the Chinese ambassador) and extracted a long cigarette, tapping the end lightly on the expensive holder. "So, my friend, are you ready to go into business together?"

DUBAI, UNITED ARAB EMIRATES (UAE)

1:15PM, AUGUST 25TH

No word. Just over twelve hours and the crew of The Jefferson Group's Gulfstream didn't have a clue what was going on. They took shifts sleeping. It was habit. Rest when you could. Luckily the cabin of the G650ER was spacious and more than comfortable. They were hooked up to airport power so it was like staying in a luxury suite. It beat living out of a Quonset hut (something the three had plenty of experience with).

Benny Fletcher was in charge of comms, checking and rechecking the upgraded network Neil Patel had installed prior to leaving the States. Every hour they radioed back to Charlottesville to let the rest of The Jefferson Group staff know they were waiting at Dubai International Airport.

Johnny Powers tapped his brother on the arm. Jim woke instantly.

"You're up," said Johnny.

"Coffee?"

Johnny pointed to the galley. "Hot and ready."

While Johnny settled in to get an hour or two of shut-eye, Jim stood and stretched, going through a practiced routine of pseudo-yoga, something one of his ex-girlfriends had taught him. Came in handy when you lived in cramped quarters.

Benny nodded to him as he entered the cockpit. "No word, sir."

Jim took the co-pilot's seat, checking the instrument panel out of habit.

"You know, Benny, if we're going to be working together you might as well get used to calling me by my first name."

"Hard habit to break."

"I know the feeling. Who would've thought we'd be sitting in this pretty bird, free to come and go as we please?"

"Most of my friends from the Army are still looking for jobs," said Benny.

"Yeah. Ain't what it used to be, being a pilot. We got lucky."

"Yeah."

"Just between you and me, I'm going to hold onto this gig for as long as I can."

Benny smiled then went back to fiddling with the radio.

Jim Powers looked out over the busy runway. In and out as aircraft came and went. Jumbo jets and private planes. The wealth in the UAE was staggering. Money everywhere.

But right now, the Marine wasn't thinking about money. He was thinking about his new boss, correction, bosses. Where were they? What were they doing, and were they okay?

* * *

KANDAHAR, AFGHANISTAN - 1:44PM AFT

Jonas Layton stood when he heard the vehicles return to Saladin's compound. He'd stayed behind with Andy, Neil and Dr. Higgins. Not much a billionaire techie could do on a raid except get in the way. He'd spent the time doing what he could via the Internet. Mostly searching in vain for something that could help the team. Zilch so far.

The armored SUVs tore into the complex. They had more dings and dents than Jonas remembered. *What the...?* Two of the heavy vehicles were smoking, roofs sagging.

MSgt Trent jumped out first, rushing to open the rear hatch. A moment later he reappeared cradling a wriggling form in his arms.

"Put me down you big ape," protested Gaucho, his arms trying to get free. There was a bandage wrapped around his leg covered in deep red.

"Shut up," said Trent, marching toward the house, giving Jonas a quick nod.

The rest of the men piled out, some wearing bandages on arms and faces. More than one man needed assistance from a comrade.

Cal and Daniel were talking. Jonas joined them.

"What the hell happened?" he asked.

Cal's eyes were hard, piercing. Jonas had seen that look before, right before the Marine had killed someone.

"We missed Farrago."

"And the wounded?"

Cal explained the scene and the incoming drones, how the rockets slammed in all around them. Somehow no one had been killed. A miracle really.

"Where's Saladin?" asked Cal.

"He went out."

"Call him back. We're pushing up the timeline."

"But what about…"

Cal leveled Jonas with a look that cut off the question. It almost made the billionaire take a step back.

"Okay."

"Let's see how everyone's doing. Daniel, figure out who can go and who needs to stay. I don't want anyone being a hero. Only those that can keep up."

Daniel nodded and walked into the house. Sometimes Jonas wished he had a friendship like the one Cal and Daniel had, or Cal and Trent, or Cal and…well, Cal and all his men. He'd agreed to help start The Jefferson Group because he'd been bored at the time, curious about what the president had in mind. As the months flew by, he'd listened and learned.

While he'd amassed an enormous fortune by the time he'd turned thirty, something had always been missing. There were plenty of so-called friends, some fair weather and some on the periphery of being close. He'd thought his lack of intimate friendships was just a symptom of his career choice, long hours and little time to be social. Sometimes he wondered if his wiring was just off and that he was destined to be one of those really rich guys who kept to themselves.

His time with Cal and his team had changed everything. Not only was Jonas doing something that was new and exciting, he was also part of a team that actually cared. In the tech and business world, plenty of people said they cared. Mostly they cared about money and the next raise.

These guys cared about their country, were willing to die for it even though they'd left their uniforms behind. They cared about the mission, proud of their hard work but never boastful. And most importantly, they cared about the men standing next to them. Race didn't matter. Background didn't matter. The only thing that mattered was the team.

Jonas wanted to be one of them. He knew being a gunslinger wasn't a prerequisite. Neil and Dr. Higgins were just as much a part of the team as the others, highly valued members with completely different skill sets.

As he watched Cal clear his weapon, methodically going through his post-battle routine, Jonas made a silent promise to himself, to whomever was listening. He would do anything in his power to use his knowledge and wealth to help these men, these warriors, these humble patriots.

WASHINGTON, D.C

5:20AM, AUGUST 25TH

The text at 4:30am was brief: *Washington Monument 0530.* Travis needed some exercise anyway. A perfect time for a jog through D.C.

There were the marathoners, fast walkers, and the interval runners. The SEAL catalogued them all as he ran, maintaining an easy sub 7-minute pace. He did three loops around the Washington Monument, even stopping to do some pushups twice, keeping his eye out for Roger Horn.

Another turn past the National World War II Memorial, workers skimming the top of the Reflecting Pool on the memorial's west side. Gray-haired veterans wearing ribbon-laden blue ball caps shuffled by despite the early hour. Travis wondered how many of the Greatest Generation came to visit on a daily basis, not a day missed. There had to be someone who kept that tally. A last vigil, praying for friends lost during and after the Second World War.

As he rounded the south end of the memorial, the Washington Monument directly ahead, something stung him on the right leg. When his hand wandered around his torso to grab the pistol tucked in the holster on his back waistband, someone whistled. Travis's head snapped that way. Sitting on a short bench was Roger Horn holding a handful of pebbles.

Travis shook his head and ran that way.

"You didn't think I was going to run after you," said Roger in greeting.

"I almost shot your dumb ass."

Roger grinned. "Yeah right."

Travis sat down next to his friend.

"Tell me you found something." Travis had been surprised by the text. He thought it would've taken days, if not weeks, for Roger to find out something about Farrago.

A nod from the former SEAL. "I don't have anything solid, like in writing, but I figured you wouldn't care. You ready for today's history lesson?"

Travis nodded. It was always something with the Horn. He and Cal would've gotten along well.

"Okay, it's not a secret that the American government helps select the next ruler of a lot of countries. That's especially true when our troops are involved and when our interests are at stake. Hell, we did it with Saddam and look where that got us.

"Anyway, specific examples aside, we, meaning the U.S. government, put a lot of effort into helping our hand-picked foreign leaders. We provide security, military training, weapons and money. Lots and lots of money. The thought goes like this: why not invest a couple billion when it'll shore up a trillion dollar industry, like oil. It's a small price to pay. Now, these appointed leaders aren't going to do it for free, like for the love of country. What most people don't know is that we take care of them. Trips, homes or straight up cash money.

"There are lots of ways to do it, sometimes we get burned and sometimes the guy does alright. We're not the only ones who do it. It's been going on for hundreds of years. Russia's doing it right now with Ukraine. That's a huge mess, by the way. But that's beside the point.

"Afghanistan was our first salvo in the War on Terror. Our troops flew in, kicked some ass, and then we set out to help the Afghan government get on their feet. You've been there, you know how many factions we've had to deal with. But through it all we needed someone we could trust, or at least a steady figure that we could count on.

"That's where agencies like mine come in. We're tasked with everything from security to administrative support. We do a lot of handholding in the beginning, then it turns into a babysitting gig, and the hope is that some day we can back away completely. Well, not completely, but you get the point. As you can imagine, it takes a lot of time and a lot of people.

"That's where guys like Farrago come in. Farrago started out with little tasks. Shuttling a diplomat in to Kabul or just delivering a handwritten note to some politician. Like I said, I can't prove this, but my buddy thinks Farrago's the main bagman now. He deals with their president directly, including coordinating funding."

"He's a courier?" asked Travis.

"No. That's part of what he does, but basically he's the one who Kingsley Coles appointed to be the guy in the background, whispering in the ear of the President of Afghanistan."

So Farrago had direct access to the current leader of Afghanistan. That still didn't explain what he wanted with Andy and Rich Isnard. Maybe Cal could figure it out.

"What do you think he's doing now?" asked Travis, stretching his arms over his head.

Roger shrugged, staring at a pair of long-legged blondes

jogging by. "With his meal ticket leaving after the election? Probably looking for a new job."

KANDAHAR, AFGHANISTAN

3:22PM AFT, AUGUST 25TH

"Yeah. Okay. Thanks, Trav."

Cal set the phone down. No one said a word as he grabbed a glass of water and gulped down what was left. His energy was fading, body and mind parched. They hadn't stopped since landing. Now the update from Travis. No time to take a breather.

"What did he say?" MSgt Trent asked. Kreyling and his men had left. It was only The Jefferson Group, Rich Isnard and Kadar Saladin.

Cal told them the same story Travis had gotten from Roger Horn. The Anthony Farrago problem just wouldn't go away.

"Isnard, is there anything you can tell us about this guy?"

Rich Isnard shook his head. "The guy's old school. Cagey. Never met anyone who likes him or really knows him."

"What about his role in Afghanistan? Is that for real?"

"We pay a lot of people. Back in Baghdad I had a nice budget for informants and guys we were trying to turn. Sometimes the mighty dollar does more than a gun barrel stuck to a thug's head."

Cal refilled his glass from the gallon water bottle sitting on the coffee table.

"Andy, anything else we should know about your operation?"

Andy had already described his mission in country, how money went missing from aid organizations and cargo mysteriously disappeared. Citizens coerced and threatened. No one had the guts to change the system. It was easier for everyday Afghans to live with it and stay out of the way.

Andy's color was back, which was good. He cleared his throat before replying in his still-hoarse voice. "Like I said, it was more of a hunch. There were rumors of backdoor deals and under-the-table cash, but I was just getting started. I don't even know Farrago, and nothing I found could even remotely link what I was looking for to the Afghan president."

"So why make the effort to keep you alive? Are you sure the guys that nabbed you didn't say anything about their plans?"

Andy exhaled. "No. They were pretty tight-lipped. No whispers. No bragging. They stuck to their routine and that was it."

"It just doesn't make sense. Why take the chance if all he wanted to do was leave the country with the money?"

A double tap honk sounded outside. Cal looked at Kadar.

"That must be my brother," he said, getting up from his chair. They'd been expecting the youngest Saladin since noon. "I will be right back, gentlemen."

When he left the room, Gaucho asked, "Are you sure we can trust this guy?" He motioned to where Kadar had been sitting as he shifted on the couch, his bandaged right leg propped up to keep his twelve stitches from pulling. The shrapnel wound would keep him out of the coming action, something Gaucho didn't want.

Cal looked to Isnard, the Middle East expert. Isnard shrugged. "Sometimes you gotta go with your gut. I think Saladin could come in handy."

The sound of the front door opening and closing cut off the conversation. Kadar walked in a moment later, followed by a younger version of himself. His brother's arm was in a sling.

Isnard and Andy stood and walked to the younger Saladin. "It's good to see you, Latif," said Isnard.

"And you as well," Latif said with a smile.

"What happened to your arm?" asked Andy.

Latif tried to raise the sling but grimaced. "I fell running away from the attack helicopters. Bad luck."

Kadar introduced his brother to the rest of the room and they took their seats. The leads were slim. Their prospects uncertain. They had Andy and Isnard back, but there was still the matter of Farrago and the Afghan president. No one in the room wanted either man to walk away, possibly with billions in tow. They had to do something, but what?

"Brother, I almost forgot to tell you. Our American friend will be arriving in..." Latif looked down at the gold watch on his wrist. "...five..."

One of the guards barked something from the kitchen.

"That must be him," said Latif.

This time Kadar stayed in his seat. The front door opened and closed for the third time in five minutes. The measured footsteps echoed as someone walked through the entryway, past the kitchen and into the living room.

The man was dressed in pared-down tactical wear, desert colored boots, matching pants and an oversized khaki shirt, perfect for concealing firearms. Cal didn't recognize the man, but Isnard did.

"You son-of-a-bitch!" yelled Isnard, jumping out of his chair.

With a grace that surprised Cal, Kadar Saladin slipped out of his seat and stepped in between the two men, a serene look on his face. Cal's hand moved to his weapon.

"It's good to see you too, Mr. Isnard," said the man in an even tone.

Isnard had his pistol gripped, for now hanging at his side. "Give me one good reason why I shouldn't..."

"Who is this guy?" asked Cal, totally confused by the spook's outburst. It was so out of character for the normally cool operator.

The stranger didn't look worried. In fact, he looked bored. He waited for Isnard to say something. Finally he did, finger straight and off the trigger, knuckles pale.

Through gritted teeth Isnard said, "This is Deputy Director of the National Clandestine Service, Kingsley Coles."

KANDAHAR, AFGHANISTAN

3:31PM AFT, AUGUST 25TH

No one said a thing. The first sound was the creaking of Andy's chair as he eased himself up. Jaw clenched. Eyes focused on one thing. Kingsley Coles.

"My names is Andrews, Mr. Coles," said Andy, his voice cutting through the silence.

"I know who you are, Major," said Coles. If he was uncomfortable he didn't show it. His face bore the exact same semi-bored expression from a moment before.

Andy focused on steadying his breathing, but his right hand shook as he stepped closer. Isnard stepped aside. Kadar stared at the Marine, taking him in, reading his cold gaze.

"This man is my friend, my trusted friend," said Kadar.

Andy's eyes moved from Coles to Kadar, and back again.

"I'm not going to hurt your friend," said Andy.

Kadar looked to Coles who nodded. Their host stepped aside, still staying within arm's reach.

"Tell me why you're here, Mr. Coles."

"For the same reason you are."

"Oh? Because I thought *I* was the one who got written off, not the other way around. My men died." His hands trembled, vision blurry.

"You knew the risks when you came to work for us."

"Risks?! Risks I can deal with. Having your chain of command believe some bullshit story about treason and turn their back on you...it's something I'd expect from the Russians, not fellow Americans."

"Then you are more naive than I thought."

The comment caused Isnard to rush forward and grab the taller Kingsley Coles by the front of the shirt.

"You arrogant prick, he almost died out there!"

Again Coles didn't flinch, face still. His hand reached down and grabbed Isnard's wrist.

"I expected this from Andrews, but you?" said Coles, his look the placid calm of a disappointed administrator.

The former Baghdad chief's gripped tightened, pulling his boss's face closer. "I suggest you start explaining yourself right now." He let go of the man's shirt and stepped back.

Still no emotion from the man who ruled over the CIA's clandestine operations. The complete lack of rebuttal threw Andy. He knew he should've been offended by the man's comments, but for some reason it made him want to listen.

"Back to my original question, Mr. Coles, why are you here?"

Coles pulled the bottom of his untucked shirt, straightening out the wrinkles from the scuffle.

"Let's get one thing straight. What I do will never be any of your concern. You work for me and...

"You mean I used to work for you," snapped Andy.

A curt nod from Coles. "Semantics. You Marines are so literal. First, your story needs mending. Not only was I responsible for having you disavowed, I was also responsible for having you kidnapped."

Andy inhaled sharply. His men. That innocent boy. Murdered because...because of what?! It was too much to digest, an unthinkable act that couldn't take hold in his brain as even being in the realm of possibility. During his time in captivity the thought that the CIA was behind the attack hadn't crossed his mind. Even when Cal told him that the Agency had disavowed him, his mind hadn't taken the deeper step. He'd just assumed that it was an isolated incident perpetuated by Anthony Farrago.

"You're thinking about your translator, your security team," said Coles. "Let me explain my rationale behind..."

"Rationale? How could you possibly begin to tell me that what you did, who you had murdered, could possibly be a good thing?"

Coles crossed his arms across his chest. "You're a historian, Major. Have you ever read about Guadalcanal?"

What the hell was this guy talking about?

"Of course," said Andy.

"Marines left behind by the Navy. Little food. Limited ammunition and air support. Those Marines were faced with overwhelming numbers of fresh Japanese troops hellbent on one thing, to push them back into the sea or kill them in the process."

Andy shook his head. "What the hell are you talking about?"

"Listening posts, Major."

"What?"

"Listening posts. You have heard of listening post, haven't you?"

"Of course. Every Marine knows what a listening post is."

"So you know that more often than not, it's the listening post that gets overrun first. They're beyond friendly lines, sometimes with little more than a rifle and a wire phone line. Two or three men. Alone. Waiting for the enemy. How many listening posts do you think were lost on Bloody Ridge? How many listening posts do you think were swallowed whole, those Marines never to be seen again? A lot. But they alerted the Marine perimeter to the enemy's disposition. The loss of a pair of Marines saved the lives of hundreds if not thousands of others. You were my listening post, Major Andrews. Just like those brave Marines huddling in some muddy hole, you had the chance to do much more good than you could ever know."

Every Marine officer, especially infantry officers, had read and reread about the bloody battles in the Pacific. Heroes like Sgt. John Basilone. Commanders like Col. Merritt Edson and Gen. Archer Vandegrift. They were Marine Corps lore, never to be forgotten. Along the way those same men made the tough calls that others couldn't. Andy had done the same when it was his turn. He'd sent lance corporals and sergeants out on patrol. Some came back in body bags on the back of MRAPs and Humvees.

While he didn't like the explanation, Andy was beginning to understand the motive.

"Were you going to leave me?" asked Andy.

Coles appraised him for a moment, then nodded as if he'd just made the decision that the man standing in front of him just might pass muster, like a Marine drill instructor leaving you alone instead of screaming at you from dawn 'til dusk. Andy was beginning to see who Deputy Director Kingsley Coles really was. Dispassionate. Focused.

"Who do you think helped you along the way? Latif Saladin waiting in Gereshk. The nomads with their Russian tanks at the check point. The helicopter pilot. And now Kadar Saladin, our gracious host. I knew Mr. Isnard would come after you even after I told him not to. Marines don't leave a fellow Marine behind, am I right?"

"But how could you have known that we'd make it out?

There were too many variables. The guards at the check point. The Hind attack..."

"Despite what Mr. Isnard thinks of me, I have every confidence in his abilities. If there was any person that could do it, it was him, and you, of course."

While Andy understood what Coles was saying, he still couldn't get past the man's academic recital, like people were mere chess pieces on a paper map. And there he was, Marine Major Andrews, the pawn of the CIA.

"And what was it all for?" asked Andy, suddenly weary of the games, tired of the intrigue. At least when you went to war as a Marine you knew who the bad guys were.

"The first target was Anthony Farrago."

"But he works for you."

Coles nodded. "True. But how better to root out a traitor than to bring him close, give him the tools to build his delusional world? The second target, who you somehow stumbled upon, is the President of Afghanistan. We believe our ally has anything but retirement on his mind, and certainly not our best interests. The operation to catch him has been in place since before I came to the CIA. Because of your capture and subsequent escape, we've been able to gather substantial information on both men. But there's still work to do."

"Like what?"

For the first time Coles's lips pursed. A sliver of worry. "We're running out of time. Farrago is obviously not telling me everything. I have no doubt that he and the president are working up to something. The questions are what, how and when."

"Wait, you don't even know what they're going to do?" asked Andy.

The slow and measured shake of Coles head told Andy everything. The master spook had hit a brick wall. He'd let the wolf out of its cage and now didn't know how to catch it in the act of stealing the farmer's sheep.

"And now you need us," guessed Andy.

Coles nodded.

Andy looked over at Isnard, then back at Cal. His former platoon sergeant nodded.

Andy turned back to his boss. "Okay, Mr. Coles. Tell us what you had in mind."

KABUL, AFGHANISTAN

5:55PM AFT, AUGUST 25TH

Another wood shaving dropped to the ground. The rough pile of flecks scattered over his bare feet, on the floor, under the bed.

Oak. His favorite. Not birch. Not pine. No. Pick the strongest. The hardest. The most unflinching.

Anthony Farrago's mind focused on the task. Whittling away in careful strokes, precise cuts. It was a habit he'd picked up as a child, under his father's tutelage.

Tutelage. That's what it was. Not loving mentorship. Not fatherly instruction. Tutelage. He was the pupil, his father the master craftsman.

His razor sharp knife dug into the hard wood, sending the tiniest speck fluttering to the floor. A shape forming, slowly but surely. No idea what it was. Better to let your mind wander, the figure carving itself, his hands merely the instruments doing the mindless labor.

Habit. Every mission, a new piece of wood, no bigger than

the size of his hand. Easier to travel with. The same every time. From the same oak. Memories in that oak. Hidden, but always there. A mirror buried deep, stubborn, built by years of shifting earth and passing rain.

He used to climb that oak as a kid. Not like other children his age, swinging from a tire or dangling from the planks of a rickety treehouse. No. That oak was a test. A monument. His challenge.

"You get up that thing and I'll consider letting you be my son," his father had said. Tony was only ten at the time. He'd looked up at that huge oak, not a handhold under twenty feet.

"How do I do it?"

"You figure it out."

He'd sat out there the rest of the day, looking up at the giant oak. A century of life staring down at him, taunting him, leering like a dirty old man with crooked arthritic arms.

The next day his training began. His two older brothers were already well ahead of him, trained by the man who'd once trained the best that America had. The men Tony had read about in his comic books, the only childish indulgence his father allowed. Spies and communism. Assassins and heroes. Not Marvel Comic heroes with superpowers. These were stories about real men. Smart. Cunning. Deadly.

Luis Farrago was fifty-five when his youngest son was born. His second wife, Tony's mother, died that night. Excessive bleeding. Nothing the doctor could do.

So Luis raised his three sons alone. He was sixty-five when he began Tony's training.

Sitting under the oak that first day, Tony stared up at his father as the elder Farrago's eyes looked off to the east, to the sun rising red on the horizon.

"I've never told you about what I did before you were born, have I?"

"No, sir."

Luis grunted, closing his eyes. "I'm going to tell you now."

He would hear the same story every year. Every time his father watched him grip that wide oak, arms and legs straining to pull himself up. Even the year his oldest brother Nick died in a training accident. Tony was twelve at the time.

LUIS FARRAGO WAS ONE OF THE FEW CIA OPERATIVES IN the late 1940s that didn't have a college education. During its time as the Office of Strategic Service (OSS), the CIA recruited the best and brightest. To men like Col. Wild Bill Donavan, the founder of the OSS, and his good friend, President Franklin Delano Roosevelt, the best and brightest were obvious. Go to Yale, Harvard, and Dartmouth and find upstanding, mostly wealthy, red-blooded Americans looking to serve their country.

But as World War II raged on, recruitment shifted to other highly qualified organizations, namely the military. That's where the CIA found Luis Farrago.

Fast forward four years and Luis was one of the men responsible for predicting North Korea's attack on its kin to the south. He spent the Korean War parachuting behind enemy lines, most times with only a pistol and a radio.

The years passed and Luis Farrago climbed the rungs of the Agency's growing bureaucracy. Like a grizzled sergeant, he wanted to be in the field. It wasn't always possible, but for the most part he spent almost forty years on the streets. Korea. Italy. Russia.

He was a go-to guy. You needed something done, someone turned, call Luis Farrago. It was after one particularly savage interrogation that the elder Farrago was "persuaded" to take a new position as a trainer at The Farm, the CIA's training facility for new recruits. Not that he had a choice. It was either that or he could pack his bags and walk off into the sunset.

It wasn't bad duty. He got to work over those whiny college kids, show them what life and the real world were really like. He often stalked his students during their time off, pouncing on them with a knife or a pistol in their homes or in a mall. He could do no wrong. It lasted two years. Then Carter was elected.

Luis Farrago's fists always clenched when mentioning the former president.

"He came in with his pansy ideas of what America should be. Weak. Changed everything."

Investigations cropped up overnight. No CIA division escaped scrutiny. Farrago's time came when three recruits complained in the right investigator's ear.

"You can't mess with these kids in their off hours," the skinny investigator had said, tapping the yellow note pad with vigor.

"How the hell am I supposed to get them ready for the Russians? You think they're not out there? They are and these kids need to know that. They need to know how to watch their backs dammit!"

He'd refused to change his tactics and the CIA was forced to relieve him of his duties, insisting on retirement.

"Come on, Luis," his boss had said. They'd known each other for thirty years. Had shed blood together. Killed together. But now his friend sat behind a desk telling him to take it like a good soldier.

"I'll walk, Karl. I'll pack my things and retire to my little farm. But mark my words, the Agency is going to see me again."

They'd watched him for years. His parting comments no doubt triggered some warning within the bowels of the CIA's info dump. But he was the teacher. He never stepped out of line, never lifted a finger in anger.

But in private he raised his sons. Not raised, trained. Methodically. Relentlessly.

He always insisted they do a stint in the military.

"Serving in the ranks will give you perspective. It'll keep you humble when they let you in at Langley."

It would happen exactly as Luis Farrago planned. After his first son's death, his second son, Michael, enlisted in the Army, completing his college degree by correspondence. Five years later he ran through The Farm, coming out the other end a spook. Unfortunately, Michael disappeared a year later during an operation in Southeast Asia.

Tony filled in, took up the slack. He was the last one left, his father's legacy dwindling.

Much to Tony's surprise, everything seemed so easy after his father's training. Miles and miles of forced marches and endurance runs. Round after round downrange with every caliber of weapon Luis could get his hands on. Days and nights prowling the streets, shadowing targets, breaking into homes and sneaking out without the sleeping owners noticing his passing.

The day Tony graduated from The Farm, he took his father's invitation to come home. By then, Luis was hobbled by bad knees and lung cancer, rarely leaving his fifty acre spread.

He was waiting under the old oak, his eyes appraising Tony as he approached.

"Are you ready to finish what you started?" his father asked.

Tony nodded, stripping off his sport coat and tie. He'd worn boots instead of dress shoes. It had been six years since he'd last tried. He was going to do it.

Tony walked up to the tree and looked up into its bare branches. It looked smaller than he remembered, but was still that hulking man, laughing down at him.

As he reached out to grab the trunk, his father smacked the back of his head.

Tony whipped around. "What?!" he dared to ask. He'd never once raised his voice at his father.

"Haven't I taught you anything? What are you doing?"

"I'm climbing the tree."

Luis Farrago shook his head. "Why?"

"You said I had to climb the tree. No tools."

Again the shake of his father's weathered head. For the first time Tony realized his father was going to die, and soon. His once taut muscles now sagged. His piercing eyes were more red than white.

"As of today, there are no rules. You do what I trained you to do, use every weapon at your disposal to kill your enemy. There are no rules."

Tony nodded. He walked around the house and returned with a chain saw. His father cackled as his son tore into the oak, inch by inch, foot by foot, until it finally came crashing down. A wicked leering man no more. Dead.

He looked to his father when he was finished. Luis Farrago said, "Now you are my son."

ANTHONY FARRAGO LOOKED DOWN AT THE PIECE OF OAK IN his hand. The same as every time before. The once nondescript hunk of wood had transformed without him knowing. He held the carved piece up to the light. A smile spread as he took in his latest creation, a snarling wolf's head.

He felt the precise etching, the perfectly grooved lines, marveling at what he'd unearthed. One last look and he stood up, walked over to the wood fire stove and its blue and yellow flames, and tossed the wolf's head in.

It was time to get to work.

KANDAHAR, AFGHANISTAN

8:11PM AFT, AUGUST 25TH

The pack of children played soccer under the flickering yellow lamplight, half of them bare chested to differentiate the teams. The taunts and shouts echoed off the walls of neighborhood compounds. There was the occasional yell from a neighbor demanding quiet.

They'd been at it for a while, neither side conceding defeat. Time was never kept. It was a neighborhood rule. Make the other team bow out first. Sometimes the match lasted well into the night, the winners trudging home in exhausted satisfaction.

It was the goalie who saw them first, men in black masks and matching uniforms. One, then five, then the streets teamed with the faceless men. The goalie didn't say a word. They never had to. He just ran. That's all it took for the rest of the kids to sprint away.

The heavily armed force cut off any escape. Front. Back. Even in the neighboring properties they swarmed. Too many to count. The relentless convergence with one focal point.

On cue, flash-bang grenades were tossed, exploding in the front and back courtyards. They moved closer, vaulting ten foot walls with ease.

Next they tossed their grenades into the house, through every opening they could find, some having to break a window to do it.

Explosions rocked the house, light and sound stunning any within. Before the dust settled, the men in black entered the building, clearing from room to room, searching with smooth swings left and right, up and down. The house was empty.

One of the first men who'd entered removed his mask with a jerk. Anthony Farrago scowled as he kicked over the IV stand next to a mussed bed, a bag of yellow fluid sloshing to the floor.

"You said they were here," he said to the man standing to his left.

"My informants confirmed that fact fifteen minutes ago," answered the man, his voice laced with indignation.

Farrago shook his head. "I don't have time for this."

Before the the team leader could react, the American's hand swept around in a backhanded swing. The concealed blade sliced through the man's throat, blood gushing out like a breaking dam.

One hand went to his throat, the other reached for Farrago. He never made it, falling forward, first to his knees, then to his chest.

Farrago ignored the spasming body and pointed to the next man in line.

"You're in charge now. Find out where they went. You have twenty minutes."

Farrago stomped out of the room, a cell phone already at his ear. "Yes. They're not here. No. I'll take care of it."

He put the phone back in his pocket, hit the street, and disappeared into the shadows, a small entourage falling in behind him.

* * *

CAL AND HIS MEN WATCHED THE WHOLE THING. THANKS to Neil, Kadar's whole house was wired with nano-cameras. The simple devices transmitted up to half a mile. They weren't close to that far away.

They'd snuck out of a hidden tunnel covered by a perfectly crafted concrete slab underneath the dining room table. It had taken every ounce of MSgt's Trent's immense strength to even get the thing to budge with a crowbar.

Ten minutes later they'd traversed the winding tunnel. Along the way their host explained how his ancestors had first used the elaborate tunnel system, spending immense time and energy on its construction. Even in the modern age, the miles of underground network came in quite useful. They were so well constructed that only the occasional upgrade was needed.

A block away, The Jefferson Group watched as Anthony Farrago dispatched the man in the very room Andy had been in less than an hour before.

"That's one cold dude," said MSgt Trent.

"Yeah," said Cal, watching as Farrago left the compound and slipped back into the night. "Who were the men with him?"

"Most likely men of the National Directorate of Security," answered Kadar.

"That's your intelligence agency?"

"Not mine, but Afghanistan's, yes."

"Who controls them? Is it a part of the military?"

Kadar frowned. "I'm afraid not. There is only one man who controls the the Directorate. The President of Afghanistan."

* * *

THE PRESIDENT OF AFGHANISTAN LISTENED AS THE MAN from the National Directorate of Security rattled off his report. He already knew the details, of course. Farrago had phoned, conveniently leaving out the part about filleting a loyal Afghan national.

"Mr. President, this American cannot be allowed to act in such a manner."

The president stood up, slamming his palm on the top of his desk. The Directorate man flinched.

"Was it not your team leader who failed?"

The man hesitated, then said, "Yes, Mr. President."

"And was he not given the order to bring in these spies at all costs?"

"Yes, Mr. President."

"Then I believe that it was well within the right of the American, my trusted advisor, to remedy the situation."

The man swallowed, his Adam's apple bobbing. "Yes, Mr. President."

"That will be all."

The man clicked his heels together in the old way, learned from the Soviets. He turned and let himself out.

The president sat down at his desk and pressed the intercom button on his office phone.

"Yes, Mr. President?" asked his male secretary.

"I am not to be disturbed for the rest of the night."

"Understood, Mr. President."

The leader of Afghanistan reached into his pocket and

retrieved a small tattered notebook. He flipped to a page halfway through, pointing to a phone number.

He dialed the number on his secure phone and waited for it to pick up. It might be a long night, but what was a couple hours of work for a lifetime of wealth?

KABUL, AFGHANISTAN

2:27AM AFT, AUGUST 29TH

It took a day to sneak out of Kandahar and into the Afghan capital. Another two days for the Saladin network and Neil Patel to do what they did best. Spies dispatched. Networks hacked.

Cal and Daniel mapped and re-mapped routes, picked apart contingencies and shored up individual responsibilities.

The plan was complicated. A lot of moving pieces. Much depended on circumstances beyond their control. They used Jonas and Dr. Higgins to hedge their bets. In addition to his other duties, Higgins prepared detailed profiles of suspects. Jonas ran analyses and predicted outcomes. Nothing was certain, but they were getting damn close.

By the time they gathered in Kadar Saladin's underground hideout, everyone knew their roles. Even Kreyling and his fellow Brits were on board. The one-eyed operator stood in the corner, arms crossed, nodding occasionally.

They were ready.

* * *

3:19AM

The bedroom door opened. Soft footfalls stepped to the four post bed. A hand reached out and nudged the sleeping form.

"What time is?" asked the President of Afganistan.

"Just after three in the morning, Mr. President. There is an urgent call for you." The night secretary handed the cell phone to the president, who'd just clicked on the bedside lamp and was in the process of sitting up.

"Yes?" asked the president into the phone. There was the sound of expelling air and the phone dropped to the mattress. The president slumped toward the edge of the bed, the secretary catching him before he fell to the floor.

More footfalls now. Four men entered. All strangers to the secretary except one.

"You have done well, cousin," said Kadar Saladin. "Now, help us take him into the next room."

* * *

8:30AM

He woke with a start. His head was throbbing, lips parched, throat aching. It took a moment to get his eyes open.

When he did, the light in the room was dim. There was a sound in the room he couldn't place, like a tape machine running on repeat. Whirs and clicks.

His chest felt heavy. He lifted the unfamiliar blanket off of his body and moved to swing his legs off the bed. That was when he noticed the tug on his arm. He looked at it. There was an intravenous line taped to it, clear fluid running the length of the tubing right up to the IV stand next to the bed.

"You might not want to do that," came a voice in English. American English.

The president turned his head and saw a man's face in the corner. It looked illuminated, like he was pointing a flashlight up at his face. He realized the man was reading from the tablet in his hands.

"Who are you?"

The man stood, sticking the tablet under his arm and making his way across the room.

"My name is Dr. Martins," said the man, his belly sticking out over his dress pants.

"Where is my doctor? Why am I here?" Again he tried to swivel around, but the nausea hit him. The doctor must have seen it, because he grabbed a plastic trashcan from somewhere and held it under the president's chin as he vomited into it.

"Better?"

The president closed his eyes and flopped back against a pillow. He could not remember the last time he'd been sick. There were perks to having the finest physicians at your disposal.

"Why am I here?" he asked again, his voice unsure.

"One of your secretaries found you on the floor of your bedroom. Your normal physician was called but never came. I was next on the list."

The president shook his head trying to remember.

"What is wrong with me?"

"It could be one of many things. We're having your blood tested now."

The thought of someone taking his blood without him knowing sent cold pricks up his spine.

"If you are here, that must mean that you are an experienced physician." His men were too smart to send him a charlatan. "What do you think that I have?"

The doctor shrugged. "Tell me, how has your schedule been? Busy?"

He tried to rise but thought better of it, the bile in the back of his throat threatening to make another appearance. "I'm the President of Afghanistan, you fool. Of course I am busy."

The doctor nodded again, nonplussed by the outburst. "In my professional opinion, you are most likely suffering from dehydration, exhaustion and possibly a virus on top of it all. Nothing a couple days in bed won't cure."

"A couple days? I don't have time for this." There were things to do, people to see, loose ends to tie up.

"I completely understand, Mr. President. However, should your blood work come back with signs of, Ebola, for example, would that not cause quite the uproar?"

"Ebola? How could I have contracted Ebola?" It was impossible. The man was lying. He searched for a phone but found none.

"Your men tell us that you were recently in contact with a delegation from Mali and another from the Ivory Coast?"

He was going to kill whoever had divulged that information.

"They were trade delegations," he lied. "But what do they have to do with me?"

The doctor nodded. "After a few phone calls from your personal staff, they found that one man from the Mali delegation and two from the Ivory Coast have contracted Ebola and are now lying in quarantine in their respective countries."

He felt like he was going to vomit again.

"It's only a precaution, but we've quarantined some of your staff as well. Despite what the media might say, there isn't much you have to worry about. As long as you don't show symptoms, all is well."

"And if I do? What then?"

Again the easy shrug from the doctor. "Then we treat you and you live the rest of your life. It's quite simple I assure you."

Just the thought of contracting Ebola made him feel like fainting. As a child he'd contracted a virus that had almost killed him. Since then he'd been diligent about keeping his hands clean, something most of his fellow countrymen cared nothing about. He'd even taken to wearing gloves, owning more than a hundred pairs that his assistant kept on hand in various hiding places. The used ones were discarded after public events.

He could deal with bullets and explosives, but invisible microbes and parasites scared him more than he'd ever admit.

"When will you know the results?" he asked, sweat forming along his hairline. He shivered.

"Later this afternoon. I suggest you get what rest you can now. I'll wake you if I have any more information."

The president nodded, his head suddenly heavy. He gathered the blanket and hoisted it up to his neck, shaking against the creeping cold. There was so much to do, so much. But his mind could not focus. All it wanted was sleep. Sweet refreshing sleep.

KABUL, AFGHANISTAN

12:52PM AFT, AUGUST 29TH

Half of government facilities in Kabul were closed. Ebola mania had hit home. Thirty seven confirmed cases according to authorities. Many wore white masks provided for free by local hospitals.

While death and disease were a fairly common occurrence in a country with substandard sanitation, Afghanistan had yet to encounter the much feared Ebola. It was all the television news could talk about. There were rumors of roving patrols smashing down doors and taking whole families away. Markets almost ceased to exist. Merchants opted to stay home with their goods to avoid contact with the public.

Like citizens in panic before a hurricane, the simmering frenzy left a dwindling supply of everyday necessities like bottled water and basic cooking goods. Both presidential candidates took to the airwaves to ask for calm. Barricades were constructed around the most vital government buildings. Hospitals were packed with masked patients exhibiting a vast array of symptoms. They pressed their children into the hands of nurses and doctors, often getting into scuffles over who would be seen first. Armed military appeared in hospital waiting rooms, some donning yellow hazmat suits. The crowds calmed.

Anthony Farrago watched it all with a detached feeling of foreboding. It had been almost a day since he'd talked to the Afghan president. It was rumored that the leader himself had contracted the disease and was being cared for by the best doctors.

The clients were calling him, asking what this meant for them. They wanted to talk to the president. They wanted a guarantee. They wanted, they wanted, they wanted.

He told them all the same thing, that he would call when he knew more, and then he hung up.

Twenty-two messages pinged on his phone. *Ping.* Now twenty-three.

Farrago wanted to turn off his phone, maybe even throw it into the next waterway he came across. But he couldn't. He still needed to talk to the president. They'd turned him away when he tried to sneak in the private entrance. New men. Men he didn't recognize. Afghans. Probably a secret cadre of men the president held in reserve.

To make matters worse, there'd been no sign of Rich Isnard and the Andrews guy. The men and their friends had disappeared from Kandahar and were probably on their way back to the States. He'd alerted his real boss, Kingsley Coles, to that fact.

Coles seemed annoyed, but he didn't press. He said he'd have U.S. entry points alerted with a takedown team on call.

The real mission was the current president and his successor. That's what he was officially doing in Afghanistan. With another leader coming, it was Farrago's job to shore up the CIA's ties with the new president with the help of the man now quarantined in the capital.

Coles did press him on that, pointing out that with the uncertainty of the contested elections, it was essential that he court both candidates. More babysitting. He was losing time along with his grip of the situation. Everything had been in place. Then the Ebola thing happened. How the hell was he supposed to contain that?

At the end of the conversation with Coles, Farrago promised a successful operation even as he planned his own escape. Time was ticking, but Anthony Farrago was nothing if not resourceful. He'd figure something out. After all, there were no rules.

* * *

1:33PM

Gaucho chuckled as another swath of hair fell from Trent's head.

"You're getting a real kick out this, aren't you?" asked Trent.

Gaucho shaved another line across his friend's head with the electric clippers. "Hey man, it's all part of the plan, right?"

"How about I shave that beard off of you. You won't be giggling like a little girl then."

"You heard the boss, I'm non-deployable," said Gaucho, pointed at his bandaged leg with his free hand.

"Whatever, man. Just hurry up."

Five minutes later, the huge Marine looked at himself in the mirror. He rubbed a hand over his stubbly head. It felt like boot camp all over again.

"Looks good, Top," said Daniel as he walked into the room.

"Yeah. If it helps the team."

Daniel smiled. "You ready to go?"

Trent nodded and brushed the stray hairs off of his shirt. "Oorah."

There would be time to clean up later. He had some new friends to meet.

* * *

5:18PM

Dr. Higgins injected another precise dose of sedative in the president's IV drip. It was important to keep a steady flow, but it was a delicate process. Every couple hours he would adjust his levels and coax his patient from his slumber. Appearances needed to be kept. The occasional advisor or minister would visit, bravely entering in a full hazmat suit, escorted by Directorate men hand-picked by Kadar Saladin.

Some asked why the doctor wasn't similarly attired and the fake Dr. Martins always insisted that being the first on the scene meant he would have contracted the virus as well. He explained that his blood was receiving the same scrutiny as the president's.

That seemed to mollify those who weren't wide-eyed at the prospect of walking into the infected space. Most said their hellos, the brief update on this or that, then left. It was important to have the president coherent during these meeting, thus the constant monitoring of sedatives.

It was almost a game to the former CIA interrogator. Not enough of the drug and the president might regain too much of his faculties. Too much and he'd look like a over-drugged invalid. No, appearances were important. The president's men had to see the president in a position of power. If not, who knew what overzealous general or political appointee might take the reins.

And so he waited, watched and administered. It was a

crucial part of the plan. But it couldn't go on forever. They had some of the president's staff on their side thanks to Kadar Saladin, but time was the enemy. There were pieces that Cal and his team had yet to put in place. More time. If they were going to make a move they needed to do it soon.

KABUL, AFGHANISTAN

This was the tricky part. There'd been no sign of Farrago. Even with help from Coles, the spook was somehow masking his location. They knew he was in Kabul, but trying to find him had turned up nothing.

Neil had found plenty of information after they'd quarantined the president, but he was still a ways from having what they needed. Under the careful extraction techniques of the undercover Dr. Higgins, every detail of the Afghan president's scheme had been catalogued, to include client information. Cal had given President Zimmer a pared down report of their findings. The orders from President Zimmer were clear, "Get me everything."

But the effectiveness of the Ebola scheme was starting to unravel. The populace was getting restless. It wouldn't be long before the simmering unease turned into protests and violence. That was not what they wanted.

The initial Ebola "patients" were chosen by Kadar and Latif Saladin. Those picked were promised lucrative payments in exchange for acting and their discretion. A crucial part of the plan was to have the Ebola scare negated before violence erupted. A simple statement explaining the unfortunate misdiagnosis would be circulated to news outlets.

That meant their time was almost gone. Jonas predicted that they might have until the end of the night, but that it would be safer to leak the news to the media before Afghanis went to sleep. The story was ready, all they had to do was whisper it into the right ears along with video clips of the patients happily leaving quarantine.

Cal paced as Neil clicked away in front of his computer. The initial stages of their plan had gone off perfectly. The Marine felt the rest of it floating in space, drifting farther away. He had to get them all, the player and the money. Oh, and there was still that little detail about grabbing Anthony Farrago.

* * *

9:37PM

The news spread from home to home with blazing speed. The Ebola patients did not have the disease. A blood lab discrepancy and shoddy follow-up was to blame. News reels showed the smiling patients leaving, waving to cameras.

Kabul exhaled a collective sigh of relief.

Farrago fidgeted with his phone, waiting for one call. He'd stopped answering it. Too many demands. He was tired of listening to their complaints.

What he needed now was a call from the president. Without him, the two successors wouldn't talk to Farrago. Not that he cared, but Coles kept checking in every hour. He had to take those calls.

A car full of celebrating men sped by, music blaring, hands

waving outside windows. Farrago ignored the revelry. His success depended on one man.

His phone buzzed. He looked down at the caller ID. Farrago smiled.

"Yes?"

"Thirty minutes."

"Okay."

Farrago shoved the phone back in his pocket and grinned.

* * *

DR. MARTINS EXTRACTED THE IV NEEDLE FROM THE president's arm and pressed the spot with a piece of gauze.

"Thank you for your assistance, doctor," he said, his spirits on the rise.

"It was my pleasure, Mr. President. I only wish that I could have diagnosed you earlier."

"It was not your fault that the technicians are incompetent."

Dr. Martins shook his head, covering the gauze with a piece of tape. "It's a shame those idiots misdiagnosed the others. I hate to think of what would have happened on the streets if the mistake had gone uncorrected."

The president frowned. "I assure you that whoever is responsible will be held accountable. You, however, are to be commended. Despite the threat, you stayed by my side. How can I return the favor?"

Dr. Martins waved the question away. "It's all part of the job, Mr. President."

"Nonsense. There must be something I can do."

Dr. Martins shook his head. "I only hope that you don't think ill of me for keeping you in quarantine because of simple food poisoning and exhaustion."

They laughed together for a moment, the Ebola scare

behind them. The president was surprised by the level of relief he felt. Death had seemed an all too real option a few hours before. That must have been the reason for the dim memories and the half-remembered dreams.

But now there was much to do. His American friend would be there soon and there would be phone calls to make, frazzled personalities to soothe. It was what he did best. He relished the thought as he eased into a pair of slippers and headed to his office.

* * *

10:49PM

The room stood and clapped when Dr. Higgins entered the makeshift headquarters.

"Oh, please gentlemen. Take your seats," said Higgins, plopping his leather bag on the floor.

"Masterful work, Doc," said Gaucho.

Dr. Higgins smiled and bowed to the small crowd. "I'm happy to say that the rest is in your capable hands."

Cal walked over and shook Higgins's hand as the others got back to work.

"Great job, doc. You sure you don't want to do that more often?"

Higgins laughed. "I think I'll let you young guns do the undercover work from now on. There were some characters who I'm sure had their doubts about my intentions."

"Okay. But if you ever change your mind..."

Higgins patted Cal on the back and went to find some food.

Cal watched him go. There weren't many as good as Dr. Higgins. The only reason he'd agreed to the Higgins's Ebola idea was that Saladin's moles were watching his back. Kadar had guaranteed the good doctor's safety, swearing on the life of his eldest son that no harm would come to Higgins.

It had given them the time and access they needed. Neil's software had churned through the reams of information, and assets had already been activated by Kingsley Coles to neutralize the threats they'd found.

They were on to the next phase of their plan. The outcome was less certain. It all depended on the actions of two men. Two men who were most likely meeting at that very moment.

PRESIDENTIAL PALACE

KABUL, AFGHANISTAN - 12:17PM AFT, SEPTEMBER 27TH

Days stretched into weeks as the contentious Afghan elections dragged on. Almost a month after the Ebola scare, all seemed to be decided. Despite his previous promise, the outgoing President of Afghanistan remained. He was the guiding hand who finally helped to bring the two presidential candidates together in compromise.

One would become the new president, while the other would be appointed the first chief executive of Afghanistan, sort of a prime ministerial role. Afghans rejoiced at the compromise, its new leadership cemented for the foreseeable future.

And so came the day for the old president to address his government, to say farewell to those he'd fought with during the last thirteen years. They'd formed a government together. They'd written a constitution together. It was never perfect, but they somehow made it work.

He stood before them on his last day to say goodbye. They looked up at him expectantly.

"Fellow Afghans, I stand before you as a man changed. Thirteen years ago we never could have imagined how far we might come. But look at us. Despite our differences, we have worked together, forged a new peace. Although the way is still clouded, and violence still looms, I am happy that we have done our part to secure the future for our children."

He went on to tell them about his fondest memories and their hardest fought victories. The time when he'd been attacked and his political opposition stood as a human shield to protect him from his aggressors. He talked of hospitals built and the education now spreading to the most remote villages. He thanked foreign allies who had helped to rid Afghanistan of the Taliban and foreign fighters. The United States was not mentioned.

Then his eyes went hard. He looked out at the crowd, taking his time to meet their gaze.

"But we must continue to be vigilant. There are those who think we are a weak country, who believe that they can manipulate our people for their own gain. The war in Afghanistan serves to benefit foreign powers. I would urge our leaders to continue questioning their motives. If peace was indeed what they intended, the United States could help us make peace."

* * *

5:10PM

Andy read the transcript of the farewell speech for the second time.

"This guy doesn't know when to quit," he said.

"You think he'd be happy with the money," said Cal, sipping from a frosted bottle of beer.

"Yeah." Andy read the speech for a third time. He knew it

was a calculated move. The guy was smart. He didn't say or do anything without a plan. They'd learned that and more from their infiltration and subsequent monitoring. From their near month-long surveillance they'd learned almost too much about the now former president. What he liked to eat. His bathroom habits. And his surreptitious business dealings.

The breadth of the man's plans were staggering. He had clients begging for help. Many he'd turned away. The speech would serve to bolster his image with those men.

But luck was on their side. As the Afghan presidential campaign dragged on, so too did their time. Only the day before Neil had cracked the final bank account in Bermuda.

Now they had names, transcripts, files, and accounts. There was only one thing left to do until they could pull the trigger.

"You sure you feel up for this?" asked Cal.

Andy cracked his neck from side to side. It had taken him longer to get back to peak form than he'd hoped. The extra time had helped. He would've hated to miss this part of the show.

"Yeah. Let's go."

KABUL SERENA HOTEL

He'd stayed up late watching the news reports from around the world. Of course the West wasn't happy. But that was fine. He didn't need them anymore.

More importantly, half of his new clients had either called or texted with their congratulations. They'd enjoyed the last minute jab against America and its allies.

It was the first day of the rest of his life, the first day in ages that he'd allowed himself to sleep in. For the past thirteen years, he'd been a slave to his schedule. No longer. He would come and go as he pleased.

The former President of Afghanistan padded to the kitchen in search of tea and a light breakfast. There were no staff on duty so he'd have to make it himself. He wanted it that way at least for a week. Privacy. He'd relished it.

Security was a necessary function, but they knew how to be invisible. That was only partly true. His favorite departure gift had come from an admirer who also happened to be a potential client in his new venture.

Much to his surprise, a distant descendant of Shaka Zulu sent him a six-man security contingent. They were huge and wonderfully black. True to custom, they wore traditional Zulu garb, including wicked spears and loin cloths, and stuck to a strict code of silence. The hopeful heir of the Zulu Kingdom (which was now part of the Republic of South Africa) mailed a note along with his "gift" explaining that he should consider the warriors his own, to do with as he pleased. They would fight to the death and never utter a word. Slaves in every sense of the word.

The former president smiled as he passed one enormously chiseled specimen and entered the eating area. They'd been with him for almost a month and he found that their presence comforted him. Oh, and the looks on the faces of his visitors! He would enjoy traveling with them, watching as those passing by stared up in wonder at the magnificent specimens.

A phone rang in the living room. The retired politician almost called for his secretary but then remembered that, for the moment, he was alone with his black sentinels. He set a teapot to boil and walked to the other room, annoyed that he had to go that far. The phone continued to ring.

"Hello?" he said into the phone.

"Mr. President?" came a voice in English.

"Yes. Who is this?"

"This is President Brandon Zimmer."

For a moment his stomach clenched. What did the American president want with him? Probably something to do with the previous day's speech. The media was going on and on about how the Americans and their president would react now that the Zimmer Doctrine was in place. But he wasn't in office anymore. He no longer had any responsibility. His nerves settled as he put on a smile.

"Hello, Mr. President. How are you today?"

"I'm fine thanks. How's your first day of retirement?"

"I cannot complain. I have to make my own tea, but it that is the price I must pay..." His chuckle was not returned from the American. "Is there something I can help you with, my friend?"

Now Zimmer did laugh. "That's an odd choice of words coming from you."

"I beg your pardon?"

"Let me explain something to you. You can say anything you want in front of cameras. It doesn't scare me. But what does bother me, what makes me want to jump through this phone right now, is what you've been doing in secret, what you've got planned for the future."

"Now I don't know what..."

"We know about the money. We know about your new business venture. We know that you killed your own coun- trymen in order to blame it on us."

That was impossible. No one knew everything except him. No. Zimmer must be bluffing.

"I do not know where you've gotten your information, but I am afraid you are mistaken."

"I'll give you one chance," said Zimmer, his voice sharp. "Admit what you've done and help us, or you're on your own."

Was it one of his partners? Anthony Farrago maybe? No. The money was hidden. He'd wet Farrago's beak with a small taste, but the vast majority could only be accessed by him. Farrago stood to lose an emperor's ransom should he be taken out of the picture. Still the worry crept into his throat. He had to force it down to answer.

"I suggest you talk to whoever has told you these lies, Mr. President. They have done you a great disservice."

No response from Zimmer. The seconds ticked by. Finally, Zimmer said, "Very well. I wish you luck."

The line went dead. He replaced the handset in the cradle

and stared at the phone. The nerve of those Americans. They always thought their money and power gave them the upper hand. Well, that would soon change. The Americans were about to have more than they could handle, and he would be the puppetmaster pulling the strings. It would be a welcome change.

His fears lifted, and he remembered his tea just as the sound of the whistling kettle beckoned from the kitchen. He turned to fetch it and almost ran into one of the Zulus who was standing right behind him, muscles glistening.

"Do you need something?" the Afghan asked, immediately remembering that the large black man would not respond. But he did.

"How was your phone call?" the man asked in American accented English.

The former president took a step back. "I...I..."

Faster than he thought possible, the giant grabbed him by the throat and lifted him off his feet. He could feel the swoon, his mind flittering toward unconsciousness. His hands tried to pry the larger man's hand off, but the anaconda grip did not relent as they moved back until he was pressed against the wall, legs flailing.

He stared at the man's eyes. They bore into him, not a shred of compassion as the sparkles turned to black spots in his vision.

He wanted to ask questions, bribe the man, anything to keep breathing. But the air never came, only the mounting pressure and fading light.

Just as the last vestiges of clarity slipped from his grasp, he heard the man say, "Semper Fi." And then the world was gone.

ALEXANDRIA, VIRGINIA

Anthony Farrago slipped into the elevator just as it was about to close. He'd checked the day before. No cameras. The building's community bulletin board said that security was being installed in the coming weeks. Not that he cared, but it was always prudent to be careful.

He got off on the fourth floor, pulling his ball cap lower as he scanned the length of the hallway. All clear. He took his time walking down the stained concrete hall, his footsteps barely making a sound.

The condo development was new, built especially for the twenty- and thirty-somethings who worked in and around D.C. It was only half sold, or so the real estate agent had told him when he'd posed as a buyer the day before.

He mentioned in passing that his friend might live in the building, an old friend from the military. When he said the name, the agent smiled and told him that his friend had actually moved in on the first of the month.

It was good to know that all of his contacts hadn't been

burned. With the disappearance of the former President of Afghanistan, his business partner, along with the billions, Farrago was left with almost nothing. It hadn't been easy sneaking back into the States.

He'd vanished, severing his ties with the CIA. According to his contacts, they were still looking for him, thinking that he may have been killed with the Afghan president.

Farrago wanted answers, and if anybody would know what had happened, it was the man he was about to visit. He pulled the keycard scrambler from his pocket and flicked the ON switch. When he came to the right door, he pressed the scrambler against the lock and five seconds later the lock disengaged. He eased the door open and stepped inside.

A shower was running. He pulled a blade from a wrist sheath. Guns were too messy. Knives were better for interrogation.

Even though he'd had the place under surveillance, he still moved from room to room making sure the two bedroom condo was empty. No signs of life except for the master bedroom. His target was getting ready for dinner, a fact his surveillance team had picked up earlier.

The water was still running when he slipped into the bedroom. There was a pistol lying on the bedside table on the opposite side of the room. Stupid.

He sidestepped into the walk-in closet as the shower shut off. A moment later, Major Bartholomew Andrews walked out of the bathroom with a towel wrapped around his waist.

Farrago made his move, sliding out of the closet and cutting off the Marine's path to the gun.

"Where's the money?" he asked.

Maj. Andrews turned. Nothing in his look said that he was surprised by Farrago's sudden appearance.

"It's gone."

Farrago took a step closer and held up the blade in his hand.

"What do you mean it's gone."

Andrews shrugged. "We took it."

This wasn't how Farrago had imagined the conversation going. Andrews was supposed to be squirming. He was supposed to fight back until the CIA veteran had to tear the information from his chest.

"Let me guess. You're probably wondering where your partner went, right? The *former* President of Afghanistan?"

Farrago almost threw the knife at the arrogant upstart. Didn't he know who he was dealing with?

There were too many questions. He'd had it all worked out. Every contingency planned to the smallest detail. The clients. The money. The overthrow.

"It's over, Farrago."

Farrago shook his head. "It's not over until I say it is."

"We've got the money. We took care of the president. And we took care of your clients. The prince in South Africa. The warlord in Somalia. The general in Ghana. I could keep going, but you know them all. I've gotta admit, you guys had a helluva plan. Teach aspiring leaders how to incite revolt and violence in order for America and its allies to come in and dump a boatload of money. Then you show them how to siphon off as much cash as they can and you guys get a hefty cut. If it wasn't so twisted, I might have been impressed. But it's over now. The racket is gone along with your friend."

Nothing made sense. But he still had what really mattered. It was what he'd been trained for, what he'd been bred for. Not by the CIA and its legions of pussy-footing government employees, but by his father, the man whose legacy was alive and well. It was all he'd thought about since joining the Agency. It was now his legacy.

He was going to be to the CIA what Edward Snowden was to the NSA.

"What do you think the world would do if it found out that the CIA, that our country, was handing out money just to get our way?" asked Farrago.

Andrew's eyes hardened. He didn't know. Farrago laughed.

"It wasn't about the money, you know. Sure that would've been nice, a good retirement. But I've got something much bigger in the works."

"And what would that be?"

Farrago almost didn't say, but he wasn't planning on leaving Andrews alive.

"I'm going to take the CIA down, piece by fucking piece. Do you know how easy it was to give you up to the Afghans? I have no idea how you got out of that, but I know the names and locations of hundreds of agents. Not only that, I also have the documentation that shows how much and which world leaders we've bribed over the last twenty years. Under that prick Coles I had access to everything. There will be congressional investigations, pressure from world leaders, implosion. By the time I'm done with it, the CIA is going to sublease its headquarters. And I'll be sitting on some sunny beach laughing my way to the next cocktail. I already have four countries bidding for the information."

"Why'd you do it?" asked Andrews. "For everything they did for you, for your family?"

"For my family?! The CIA hasn't done anything for my family! They ran my father out. They killed my brother. You tell me exactly how they've helped my family."

"I feel sorry for you."

"You can go fu— "

The words stuck in his throat. He arched his back at the shooting pain, pressure in his chest, then came the burning and the tearing torment. Farrago tried to turn but he couldn't, like he was pinned in place. He looked down, his eyes bulging. Five inches of blood-lined metal were sticking out of his chest. He watched as the first drops fell to the floor.

The knife slipped from his hand, clattering to the hardwood floor as his hands grasped for the metal poking out of his shirt. Sharp cold steel, like a sword. The edges cut into his hands, the pain excruciating as he tried in vain to pull it out.

Without warning, the blade slid out of his body, the release turning him weirdly. He spun to face his attacker, blood seeping into his mouth, metallic and warm on his tongue. His knees wanted to buckle, but he willed them to keep standing, wobbling from side to side.

His mouth dropped open when he saw the man holding the blade.

"You!" he wanted to say, but the only thing that came out of his mouth was a gush of blood.

"Your services are no longer required," said the man, pulling the blade back and then thrusting it into Farrago's heart.

One beat. Two beats. And then Anthony Farrago collapsed into nothingness.

ANDY WATCHED FARRAGO FALL TO THE FLOOR AS THE BLADE slipped out of him.

Kingsley Coles bent down and wiped the long blade on a clean part of Farrago's shirt. Once satisfied, he slid it into some unseen sheath behind his back. His face looked unconcerned, like he'd just taken out the garbage.

"I thought Isnard was coming," said Andy.

"I insisted on doing this myself. He was my responsibility," said Coles, readjusting his shirt like he'd just finished up in the men's room. "Have you considered my offer?"

Andy nodded.

"And have you made a decision?" Coles took a step back to avoid the blood that was spreading from Farrago's wounds.

"I have."

"And?"

"I accept."

"Good. Have you decided where you'd like to start? Back to the Middle East, or perhaps a position with Mr. Isnard?"

Andy shook his head. "I'd like to come work for you."

Cole's eyebrow rose followed by an amused smile, the first Andy had seen. "And why would you assume that I'm hiring?"

Andy pointed at the body on the floor.

Coles nodded. "Very well. Take the weekend. You start on Monday."

"Thank you."

"You may not be thanking me in a week. One last question. I've heard that you don't like being called by your given name. I don't do nicknames, so what should I call you?"

No hesitation. "Mr. Andrews."

Coles blinked. "Very well, Mr. Andrews. Here's the number of the man who will take care of Mr. Farrago's body. He should have things cleaned up by the time you get back from dinner." Coles set a card on the bed, looked down at the body one last time, and left the room.

After he heard the front door close, Andy looked at himself in the full length mirror and said, "What have you gotten yourself into now, Mr. Andrews?"

EPILOGUE

True to form, the Marine Corps Birthday Ball at 8th & I was an extravagant event. Marines in dress blues mingled with guests in tuxedos and danced with dates in elegant gowns. The booze flowed freely, and the camaraderie created an electric hum in the room, accompanied by the thumping bass coming from the oversized speakers.

The cake was cut and served to the youngest and oldest Marines present, and the commandant's message was played even though the commandant was in attendance, a last minute change.

Cal hadn't been to the Ball since leaving the Marine Corps. He was one of the men wearing a tailored tux instead of his blues. Diane Mayer had come as his date and dazzled the room in her sapphire dress that twirled as MSgt Trent spun her on the dance floor. Cal laughed as the huge Marine dipped her almost to the floor, then guided her up like Fred Astaire. No doubt about it, Top had some moves.

The Marines of The Jefferson Group had come as guests of General McMillan, USMC, the Chairman of the Joint Chiefs. He wasn't there to overshadow the event, but he'd explained to Cal that he wanted to support his old friend, Gen. Winfield, USMC, who'd just taken over the helm of the Marine Corps.

While Cal had first declined the invitation, the incessant prodding from MSgt Trent changed his mind. It was good to be back with real Marines. The feeling spread as he watched his friends enjoy themselves. Even Daniel was dancing.

Cal felt a tap on his shoulder. He turned to find a Marine captain standing with his hands behind his back. He wore the golden ropes of a general's aide-de-camp. Cal could never remember how many meant what, but he did know that more ropes signified a higher rank of general. This guy had a bunch.

"Sir, can you follow me please?"

"Are you sure you've got the right guy?" asked Cal, glancing over his shoulder to where Diane was jumping up and down with the rest of the crowd to MC Hammer's "U Can't Touch This".

"Yes, sir, Mr. Stokes."

Cal drained the rest of his whiskey and followed the Marine out of the ballroom and down a long hallway. A lance corporal and his date were making out in a shallow alcove, lipstick smeared all over the Marine's face.

Some things never change, thought Cal.

They went up a flight of stairs and came to a closed door.

"They're waiting for you in there, sir."

"Who?"

The captain had already done an about-face and was marching back the way they'd come.

Cal shook his head and opened the door.

It looked like a smoking lounge in a swanky country club, dim light coming from bronze sconces on the walls. Cushy leather armchairs here and there. No fire in the fireplace. Two of the seats were occupied. The men rose from their seats when Cal entered the room.

"Thanks for coming, Cal," said Gen. McMillan. He was holding a water glass that was three quarters full of some dark liquid.

"Not a problem, general," said Cal.

"Have you met General Winfield?" said McMillan, pointing with his glass at the Commandant of the Marine Corps.

"I have not had the pleasure." Cal stuck out his hand. "General, my name is..."

"Staff Sergeant Calvin Stokes, Junior," finished the Commandant. His grip was firm. He held Cal's hand for a long moment. "You look like your dad."

It wasn't uncommon for Marines to know his father. At the time he'd left the Corps, Colonel Calvin Stokes was destined to be a general. There'd been talk that he'd pick up three, maybe even four stars one day. He'd given it all up for his family, for Cal.

"That's what they tell me, sir."

"He was a good man. I worked for him. He was my first company commander. Kept me out of trouble as I tried to figure out how to lead Marines." Winfield let go of Cal's hand and motioned to one of the leather armchairs. "Can I get you anything?" he asked, pointing to a row of bottles on a rolling cart.

"Whatever you're having is fine, thanks."

Cal took his seat while Gen. Winfield dropped ice cubes in a tall glass and then filled it halfway. Cal wondered how many of those the two generals had had together.

The commandant handed the glass to Cal and took his seat.

Gen. Winfield raised his own glass and said, "To the Corps."

Cal and Gen. McMillan repeated the toast and took respectful sips from their glasses.

"I hear the president's been keeping you busy," said Winfield.

Cal eyes snapped over to McMillan.

"The president gave me the okay, Cal," said McMillan.

"I'm sorry. I didn't mean to put you on the spot, son. Maybe me and Mac have had a couple too many. Wouldn't be the first time, eh, Mac?"

Gen. McMillan tipped his glass then took a healthy swallow in reply. Cal amended his previous thought. These two weren't tipsy, they were hammered. What the hell was that all about? Maybe it was just the celebration.

"It's okay, general. Yes, I have a certain...arrangement with the president."

McMillan chuckled and took another swallow of his drink.

Gen. Winfield set his glass down and put his hands together, palm to palm. His face sagged and he suddenly looked tired, older than when Cal had walked in the door.

Cal waited.

Winfield's eyes refocused on Cal. "Do you think, if the situation warranted it, do you think that the president would be okay with you helping me with a little...problem?"

"I don't see why not. I take it that this is something you want to keep out of normal channels?"

"It is."

"And your staff or the investigative services like NCIS couldn't help?"

"I'm afraid not."

"Then why me, general? I'm just a dumb grunt with a small team. I'm sure there are a lot of people that are way more qualified to do whatever you need. Besides, you don't even know me."

Gen. Winfield sat up, his eyes now boring into Cal's. "I need a Marine who can get things done. I need a Marine who remembers where we came from. I need a Marine who still believes in honor, courage and commitment. From what Mac tells me, *you're* that Marine."

Gen. McMillan nodded and drained the rest of his glass. He rose to refill it. "We've been through our options, Cal, and you're it."

What the hell were they talking about? Here were the Commandant of the Marine Corps and the Chairman of the Joint Chiefs, and with all their resources they were left with him?

"I'm sorry gentlemen, maybe you can explain the situation," said Cal.

"Tell him, Scotty," said McMillan.

Gen. Winfield nodded. "I don't know how to put this, and you'll probably think I'm crazy...but I think—"

"We think," interrupted McMillan.

"We think there's an ongoing operation to discredit the Marine Corps."

"For what purpose?" asked Cal.

Another look passed between the two generals. He'd seen that look plenty of times before, two Marines getting ready to take on an overwhelming enemy force, one or both likely to get killed.

Gen. Winfield said, "We believe that come this time next year, there will no longer be a United States Marine Corps."

* * *

I hope you enjoyed this story.

If you did, please take a moment to write a review ON AMAZON. Even the short ones help!

GET A FREE COPY OF THE CORPS JUSTICE PREQUEL SHORT STORY, *GOD-SPEED*, JUST FOR SUBSCRIBING AT CG-COOPER.COM

TO MY BETA READERS:

Sue, Cheryl, Susan, Mike, Marc, Don, Doug, Robert, Duane, CaryLory, Nancy, Glenda, David, Kathy and Jim. You guys are awesome. Thanks for keeping me humble.

ALSO BY C. G. COOPER

The Corps Justice Series In Order:

Back To War

Council Of Patriots

Prime Asset

Presidential Shift

National Burden

Lethal Misconduct

Moral Imperative

Disavowed

Chain Of Command

Papal Justice

The Zimmer Doctrine

Sabotage

Liberty Down

Sins Of The Father

Corps Justice Short Stories:

Chosen

God-Speed

Running

The Daniel Briggs Novels:

Adrift

Fallen

ABOUT THE AUTHOR

C. G. Cooper is the *USA TODAY* and AMAZON
BESTSELLING author of the CORPS JUSTICE novels
(including spinoffs), The Chronicles of Benjamin Dragon and
the Patriot Protocol series.

Cooper grew up in a Navy family and traveled from one
Naval base to another as he fed his love of books and a
fledgling desire to write.

Upon graduating from the University of Virginia with a
degree in Foreign Affairs, Cooper was commissioned in the
United States Marine Corps and went on to serve six years as
an infantry officer. C. G. Cooper's final Marine duty station
was in Nashville, Tennessee, where he fell in love with the
laid-back lifestyle of Music City.

His first published novel, BACK TO WAR, came out of a need to link back to his time in the Marine Corps. That novel, written as a side project, spawned many follow-on novels, several exciting spinoffs, and catapulted Cooper's career.

Cooper lives just south of Nashville with his wife, three children, and their German shorthaired pointer, Liberty, who's become a popular character in the Corps Justice novels.

When he's not writing or hosting his podcast, Books In 30, Cooper spends time with his family, does his best to improve his golf handicap, and loves to shed light on the ongoing fight of everyday heroes.

Cooper loves hearing from readers and responds to every email personally.
To connect with C. G. Cooper visit
www.cg-cooper.com

Made in the USA
Middletown, DE
22 June 2020

10508006R00137